D0948175

*Clarise
Cumberbatch
Want*
to Go Home

Clarise Cumberbatch Want to Go Home

JOAN CAMBRIDGE

TICKNOR & FIELDS • NEW YORK • 1987

Library of Congress Cataloging-in-Publication Data

Cambridge, Joan.
Clarise Cumberbatch want to go home.

I. Title.
PR9320.9.C26C58   1987   813   86-14526
ISBN 0-89919-403-6

Printed in the United States of America

S 10 9 8 7 6 5 4 3 2 1

The author is grateful for permission to quote from the following works:

Page vii *For My People* by Margaret Walker, first published in 1942 by Yale University Press. Lines reprinted here with permission of the author.

Page 120 "If I Ruled the World" by Cyril Ornadel and Leslie Bricusse, © 1963 by Chappell & Company, Ltd. Published in the U.S.A. by Chappell & Company, Inc. International copyright secured. All rights reserved. Used by permission.

Page 188 "How Do You Keep the Music Playing?" Music by Michel Legrand and lyrics by Alan and Marilyn Bergman, © 1982 Warner Brothers Music Corporation. All rights reserved. Used by permission.

The publisher has made every effort to locate all owners of material reprinted here and to obtain permission to reprint it. Any errors or omissions are unintentional, and corrections will be made in future editions if necessary.

Chapter 1 of this book appeared in somewhat different form in the *Antioch Review* (Fall 1984): 465–77.

Posthumously,
this book is dedicated to
JULIAN HUDSON MAYFIELD,
husband, teacher, friend.

for my people everywhere
. . . singing their sad songs, their dirges . . .
— *Margaret Walker*

One

Clarise reach New York early March when it cold like dog-nose and she shivering and lonely. It woulda been all right if all she come here for was to see the place; how you could have plenty plenty furnitures and clothes and things and eat anything you want to eat. How you could buy long long motorcar like what Harold and Leonie posing in front of in the snapshots that she-de-Leonie send home to show-off with.

But no.

Clarise come here with a heavy heavy heart. More heavy than her grip with her few things in it. Cause she *swear* she not going home again till she find Harold and show him how he making a big mistake if he think that America and a wild woman like Leonie is all this life have to offer.

Men does forget too easy . . .

1

Clarise talking to herself and moving-up with the people in the long long line.

. . . You always have to keep reminding them, she thinking in her mind and just following the people in front her, like a child.

She seeing lights lights lights all over the place. Saying to herself:

Lawd! Is why they have to have so much lights? I wonder is what is de price of they electric bill every month?

Then Harold cross her mind.

Is why he leave me, eh? Clarise asking herself and moving up up up with the people in the long long line. Is why he had to do that to me?

She soon find herself in front the whiteman in the cage behind the counter and she give him her passport like when she was leaving Guyana and like when the plane stopover in Barbados and she take a walk in the airport. But what this man saying now?

"What you say, mister?"

"You're in the wrong line, ma'am."

"De wrong line?"

"Yes, ma'am. This is not your line."

"Not my line? Ohhh . . . I thought you could go anywhere, that I could stand-up in any li —"

"That line over there," the man say, and he pointing behind his back with his big-finger.

Clarise look. And is then she see that she really and truly get in the wrong line with all them whitepeople who begin to board the plane as soon as it leave Guyana. When the plane hit Trinidad a few get on with they face red red from the sun.

But see when it reach Barbados? Lawd! Clarise never see so much whitepeople in one place for a long

2

long time, since long before Independence. She forget . . .

Is Harold. Is he make so. If her mind didn't so full-
up with him she wouldn't do stupidness so. Clarise
shame. She shame shame shame. Cause the people all
looking at her now cause they see how she get in the
wrong line like a fool, like a dunce. Cause look! Is
everything write-up big pon the signs all over the place.

"This line is for citizens and residents," the man
saying while he pointing to the sign behind his back.
"You should be in the line over there, for visitors."

He like he vex. He sounding vex? Clarise not sure.
But she certain that she getting on the people behind
her nerves cause they scraping scraping they foot pon
the ground and shifting shifting theyself.

"Thanks, mister," Clarise say to the man. "Thanks.
I'm sorry," she say, and she hang her head. But is not
for the man sake she shame, cause he done forget her
long time and busy stamping somebody else passport.
Is the people in the line she shame for. Cause they all
looking at her like if they saying to theyself, "Just look
at her with her presumptuous self. Is good she now have
to take her place in her rightful line."

Poor Clarise. She fetch herself over to the other line,
dragging the canvasbag Miz Goring lend her pon the
ground with her foot. Poor Clarise. When she reach-up
to the next man in the other cage? She busy telling
herself:

Clarise, f'Godsake! Catch y'self, chile. Stop thinking bout Harold a lil bit and settle y'self so you could
answer de man questions good, hear?

She answer the questions: Why she come to America? How long she intend to stay? Is who she staying
with? Not one damn thing she tell the man is truth, but

3

she answer his questions good he can't tell is not truth. Is how he going to know is lies, eh?

So the man make BAM! with the stamp and tell Clarise is all right, she could go now.

Ohhh God!

Is what he mean, eh? He mean she in America? She free to get out the airport in New York?

America? She Clarise? In America?

Clarise Cumberbatch? Countrygirl from Beterverwagting? From BV? In America?

Clarise who never never dream she could ever be in America although she always dreaming bout America . . . in America?

AMERICA?

Pinch y'self, Clarise girl! Pinch yourself and see if is true is you in America in truth.

Clarise pinch herself and all of a sudden she forget is she in America. All she can think bout is why she come here in the first place — cause Harold leave her. The man just ups heself justso! Without so much as a "Ta-ta, dawg!" and he gone off behind his sweetwoman Leonie although he promise Clarise and he show her by staying home every livelong night for two whole years that he and Leonie break-up, done, finish! Clarise was happy for straight two years.

Then BLAM!

One night she come home from a picnic at the airbase — is what they calling it now? Timehri Airport, where all the planes taking off for America.

Was a picnic by the Redwater Creek. Was a nice picnic, the big-people church outing. The children Sunday-school outing is on Easter Monday so they could fly they kites and so. But this big-people outing is on August Monday, Emancipation Day, holiday like the ole people use to celebrate when Clarise was a lil girl and she use to hear her grandmother and father singing:

> fust of August come again
> hurrah me ganga!
> God bless de Queen in England
> who give all o' we FREE-DOM!

Was a nice holiday day. Sun hot hot like fire and all the big-people playing in the sand like children. Even the parson wife that was visiting from Scotland was rolling in the sand and laughing-up and playing that day. Was hopscotch and skipping and Miz McDougal was playing with them:

> Take
> take
> take-down, take-down
> take
> take
> take-down, take-down

and:

> There's a colored girl
> in the ring
> tra la-la-la-la
> there's a colored girl
> in the ring
> traa lala lala
> for she love sugar
> and I love plum!

And when they get to the part that say, "Skip cross the ocean"? Whoever was in the ring had to go skipping round it. But the sweetest fun that day was when they get to the part in "There's a colored girl in the ring"

5

when Miz McDougal was in the ring and was time to wind her body in time. Everybody nearly bust they sides laughing, cause Miz McDougal look funny!

Y'see when they say:

> show me y'motion
> y'think I making fun?

was sweet sweet fun with Miz McDougal that day.

But the body who really surprise everybody was Miz Van Rossum.

Eh-eh!

Miz Van Rossum is over eighty years old. Ain't nobody who don't know that, although Miz Van herself would never admit it, and pon a Sunday she coming to church dress-up high high in mini skirt over her knee and she still riding her bicycle up and down the East Bank Road. Is everybody know Miz Van been down here long even though she looking so good and spritely with herself.

Eh-eh! But m'dear? Y'see when they were playing "There's a colored girl" and Miz Van turn come and she get in the ring? If you did see her *moves!* Eh-eh! That ole lady Miz Van could properly *do* herself. Eh-eh!

> show me y'motion
> y'think I making fun?

Look! Miz Van take off like a trigger and she wind like a ball of twine. Everybody had to loose hands to clap her and they saying, "Wine wine wine, Miz Van! OIE! OIE! OIE! Miz Van."

And when they stop clapping her? They all hugging her and kissing her, saying, "Ohhh! Ohhh! Miz Van? Miz Van, we didn't know you still have so much ginger so!"

6

Cause was nice to see that ole lady move. Was really nice. And as they all agree, some of them born-weary and grow-tired young people these days would glad to have moves like her. Miz Van even show them how she could bite her big-toe still and when everybody take a try they soon find out that it not so easy when the bones get ole and brittle.

Was a nice day. Was sweet sweet fun.

They eat roti-and-curry and chowmein. They had conki and mauby sourie drink and five-finger drink and other nice things. Then going home on the bus they laugh it over and talk it over.

Was strange.

Suddenly Clarise coulda hear a pin drop and she find herself again in another sweet ring-play, this time with sleep creeping up pon them all together and one at a time through the bus like in some kinda hide-and-seek game. Miz Rawlins laugh-out when she wake up and find that sleep catch up with her and she didn't even know.

"Is good is good is good! Is nice to have sweet fun so," Miz Heyliger say, and Miz Van open her mouth to talk but the words get snatch away same time with Miz McDougal head getting toss aside. Her neck coulda break, but she wake up laughing ha-ha-ha!

Ready-mister-catcher-can't-catch-me! Clarise say in her mind. Cause she playing her own game with sleep and she know what it trying to do now is to steal her memory of that nice day to make dreams. Just then, just when sleep catch up with all the rest and Clarise winking-up her eye and saying in her mind, I in *gool* now! Just when the whole bus quiet and all she can hear is the sound of the engine and the driver coughing through his cigarette smoke, Clarise say:

7

"I wonder if everybody thinking de same thing I thinking? That my husband and children going be waiting for me to come home and I wonder if they hungry and what I going cook for dinner?"

She thought she say it in her mind, to herself. She didn't know she say it hard in the bus, till she hear everybody laughing-up and saying, "Y'know is sleep I just come out de sleep right this minute and thinking de same thing?"

Miz O'Lonza say she going to warm-up the pepperpot and give her husband and they all agree that pepperpot is a nice thing to have in the house for nights like tonight when push-come-to-shove.

But Miz Blackett say, "If them children don't want to eat lil bread-and-butter and climb in they bed nice and peaceful and thankful? They will have to starve."

Ow ow ow! Clarise saying to herself now in the middle of her memory of what Miz Blackett did say that day bout five years ago.

Dear God, my God, you who just belong to me alone. You who for Clarise. Please take care of him. What he looking for? Help him to find it and if he get loss? Help me to find him so I can show him de way . . .

Eh-eh! Is a merry-go-round de grips coming off from?

Clarise stand-up in the baggage-claim area staring and waiting. Her mind going round with the merry-go-round with all the passengers grips pon it . . . To that day, then the night after the picnic. To when Miz Blackett say so bout the bread-and-butter and her children and everybody, every single body beside the driver and Miz McDougal shout out together, "Y'see? Y'see, Miz Blackett? Miz Blackett, y'see how you lucky you don't have husband to worry bout?"

But Miz Blackett ain't pick-she-teeth and is justso

the bus get quiet again cause everybody coulda bite they tongue, cause they remember, they all remember how Miz Blackett nearly die when her husband die.

Clarise put her hand to her heart. Not that for Harold, please. Not nothing so. Not now . . . If Harold was to die? De sky would fall in, that's all. De sky would fall in.

But how you know he not dead already, Clarise? How you — ?

Nooooo! Please . . .

Is so Clarise stand-up in Kennedy Airport waiting for her baggage and going over her life in her mind.

That time when Leonie sidetrack him? That first time? She didn't know what to do. At first she didn't believe, but then she find out that Harold had another woman with her and that the woman was Leonie? At first the shock nearly kill her.

Eh-eh. That woman come inside her house posing as Stretch, one of Harold friends' girlfriend. Clarise cook for them. She feed that woman, she entertain her. Eh-eh! Look! When Clarise find out? She was so vex she didn't know what to do. She say she not going tell Harold nothing till she find out the story good first. Cause she still telling herself is not true even though people bringing the news. Is so they bringing the story every day.

When Harold come home late one afternoon? Next day Clarise put her pot pon the fire and wait . . . Somebody going bring the news: Harold and Leonie been to matinee at the Metropole Cinema or Astor or Plaza. This time Harold done tell her how he had to work late.

Watch de grips coming now. Ow Lawd! I hope that lil string tie-up mine ain't bust. That grip disgraceful enough as it is . . .

You shoulda hear them news bringers:

9

Eh-eh, Miz Cumma? "Clarise chile, I see your husband and he sweetwoman in matinee. If you did see them how they hugging-up and loving-up. Well I tell you!"

They only *too glad* to bring the news and although Clarise glad in a way to hear how her life going, the people getting on her nerves.

Is Zephrine — the same Zephrine who just done get baby by a boy the police pick up cause they find him selling trackshoe and hardpants he thief from them barrels coming in from America at Sprostons Wharf where he was working. The police find that boy with over *twenty thousand dollars* pon his person but Zephrine baby didn't even have not one shimmie to put on when it born. But hear she-de-Zephrine! Hear her:

"*My* husband coulda make heself so fast? Have woman big and broad with me? And he walking bout *braddar* with she so everybody could see? Is so he going have another woman with me? No! Not so! Never-de-day!"

And Gertrude, too. Hear Gertrude:

"Was me? I woulda throw his ass out de house early o'clock!"

This time everybody know how her husband done throw heself out her house cause since last year he disappear in the bush. He say he woulda take her but he ain't walking with no *cross* to go to the gold bush.

"Eh-eh! Every afternoon that wretch does stand-up outside your husband workplace waiting for him to leave work! You must go, girl, you will see for y'self. I never see nothing so, Lawd!"

". . . and he was towing her pon his bicycle, by Kitty seawall . . ."

". . . and she have on a green-and-red flowerdress

and he have on his desertboots you did buy for his birthday present when you give that party . . ."

The women with the news living pon Clarise bones till she decide to go and see for herself. She didn't tell Harold *a word* about what she hear. She just put on her clothes one afternoon and go and stand-up by the lighthouse gate cross the street from the Ministry of Works yard where Harold working. Clarise reach there round half-past-three. Harold working till four. She know that.

By quarter-to-four, guess what? Guess is who she see coming down the road!

Is Leonie! Is Harold sweetwoman dress-up high in a big-eye flowerdress and she flouncing up to the gate-man and talking to him like if they is buddy buddy friends. And then . . . ?

To this day Clarise can't say how that woman manage to spot her standing there under that tree side the gutter by the lighthouse gate waiting quiet and peace-ful. Cause all she go there for was to *see story* with her own two eyes. When she see Leonie she say to herself that that is not enough and she must stand-up there and see what going happen, if Harold going come out and go off with Leonie.

Clarise go there to *see* story, not to *make* story.

But when she-de-Leonie turn round and she and Clarise eye make four right cross the road from the gateman house all the way to the lighthouse bridge?

Eh-eh!

Is cross Leonie crossing the road. Is walk she walking up to Clarise and cuss she cussing out poor Clarise. Well yes, Clarise! If you can't believe your eyes, now what bout your ears?

Eh-eh! Well what is this at all?

Clarise watching Leonie coming down pon her, cussing-up and carrying on bout how she Clarise got de ring but she Leonie got de man.

Clarise watching and saying to herself:

Lawd! You just look at my trial this good afternoon? You know that I shoulda cut this woman tail long ago since I hear bout her? But cause I love peace so much, I play like if I don't care. Now watch! Watch that ole-time whore, who take her belly make graveyard, coming cussing me down for my own husband? I standing here minding my own business and is come Leonie coming to beat me? Well!

Clarise put her hands pon her hips. She ain't say a word to Leonie. She just plant her hands pon her hips and her two feet solid in the earth where it soft from the rain that just over. Clarise waiting and she saying in her mind:

Lawd! You know Clarise is a peaceful soul, but still! Tickle me and I will wine! So thou knowest, Lawd, that if Leonie only take you out her thoughts today and put so much as her lil finger pon this sinful body of mine? Going be *cat-piss-and-pepper,* Lawd! It going be *cat-piss-and-pepper* this afternoon!

But Leonie, she shoulda take one look at Clarise face and realize she was in for a good cut-ass that day. She didn't have to watch how the woman stand-up with her two feet apart and her hands pon her hips. She just had to watch how Clarise black face set-up like when all the clouds turn the same dark color in the sky and you know, even if you be the smallest chile, you know that rain going kick dust soon.

But no! Not Miz-lady-Leonie. She walk right down the parapet, up to Clarise, and stand-up jooking her lil finger in Clarise face.

"Is why you so stupid, eh? You can't see de man

don't want you? Is what you come here for? Like you ain't know all you got is de ring? I got de man, man. Why you don't give up! Rest up! You done loss already. Is my intention to be Mistress Cumberbatch."

Eh-eh! If you did see Leonie airing off that day. Is a good thing plenty people not on Water Street by the lighthouse that day, cause Clarise is a body don't like no brawling in the streets with big-crowd like some circus show.

And she don't go looking for trouble. But if it come looking for her like Leonie come airing off herself in front her now?

Clarise sweep Leonie hand out her face. She don't say a word, she just brush Leonie hand away like if she saying shoo-fly-don't-bother-me-and-you-ain't-company . . .

Eh-eh! Is who tell her to do that?

Miz Leonie let fly with one big-cuff straight to Clarise face BOP! and is justso she Leonie end up sitting down in the nasty gutter by the lighthouse there, crying and cussing-up and carrying on while Clarise walking away from there. When she hit Clarise? Clarise just take her by the scruff of her neck . . . she just grabble a handful of Leonie nice flowerdress by the neck.

"Loose me! Loose me, you ugly black bitch!"

Leonie fighting-up and cussing-up and Clarise thinking in her mind while she dunking Leonie head in the gutterwater that them redwomen like Leonie with they dirtypowder complexion does really feel that that is all they need in this life.

She will soon know who black and ugly when I finish dunking she in this stinking water, Clarise say to herself.

Clarise hear a noise by the gateman house over the road and out the corner of her eye she see him leave and gone running. She know he gone to call Harold, tell him his woman and his wife outside pon the road fighting-up by the lighthouse gate. But this ain't going take long, Clarise say to herself, dipping Leonie head in the water again, not even worrying bout the dirty water splashing-up pon her clothes when Leonie kicking-up in the gutter.

Then when Leonie make a big-struggle Clarise suddenly loose her and turn and walk away. She don't even look back and she don't hurry either. She just walk away slow slow with Leonie bawling and trying her best to draw a crowd.

Clarise don't even look back to see if the watchman find Harold and if is he Harold going come to pick his woman out the gutter. She hearing the loud talking but she ain't even listening, she only walking away.

Clarise just catch the seawall road and point her head straight home with the seabreeze fanning her face and her mind working like a clock (cause she see for herself now and she have to face Harold later), Clarise walk the whole seven miles till she reach BV.

Harold reach home before her that afternoon and before Clarise can open her mouth he first start talking: Is lies is lies is lies. Is *all* lies! What Clarise mouth-foremost friends tell her? Is lies! What she think Leonie go to his workplace for? Is lies! What they say they see? Is lies! What Leonie tell her that very afternoon at his workplace? Is lies! Everything is a whole-pack-of-lies, and Clarise? She is a madwoman if she can believe all them lies.

"Don't take lead-up, Clarise," Harold say. "Is lies!"

Next day Miz Goring, Clarise neighbor, call her over her house and advise her to put a stopping to the whole thing once-and-for-all.

"Go see the readwoman, Miz Cumma."

Miz Goring tell Clarise that that time when her husband giving her plenty plenty worries? She went to see that same see-far woman she recommending to Clarise and she would tell anybody with man-worries to go see her. But Clarise tell Miz Goring that she don't believe in no obeah, and her mother before her never believe in it either, so to go to obeahwoman now? Just cause she have lil trouble with her husband?

"Is not *obeah*, Clarise. But evenso is obeah! If it will help? Why not? She help me, chile, I ain't shame to say. And if anybody want to call it obeah that is *they* problem. Me and my man we living happy and nice now."

Clarise take Miz Goring advice, cause is true that lady husband don't leave her side at all at all. Lately Mr. Goring home all the time early after work in the afternoon, pon a Friday night and Saturday night and Sunday too, home all day long. Is right home in his house he having the sessions with his friends and when they leaving and they say to him, "Come, Phillo boy! Lehwe go by Thirst Spot and fire one more, Mr. Goring saying no, he had enough. Or if he go to the rumshop with his friends? He would soon come home again.

And Miz Goring? She only laughing laughing all the time like a lil girl. And her face and her cheeks full-out again and she get back all the nice thick skin that she did loss when she had worries plus she walking bumptious-like again.

Yes, mustbe that! Is the obeahwoman make so. Is only when Miz Goring tell her that Clarise know what change Miz Goring life.

So Clarise take the advice. She go to see the readwoman and she follow *all* her instructions.

First thing she tell her is Clarise can't blame Harold for what happening cause is not his fault, is *do* Leonie *do* he and what Clarise have to do is get a *stronger work* to counteract Leonie work. The obeahwoman tell Clarise she have to noint her with oils and clean out her house with the same oils and set up a light to draw Harold back home.

"Your life confuse," she say to Clarise. "You need some peace in your life."

She give Clarise a list with six oils and tell her to go to the drugstore and get them and bring them to her. Clarise go to ole-man Beresford drugstore in the market cause there is where she does always buy her drugs. She call him aside so the other customers won't hear cause although the government make obeah legal she for one still shame to let people know she dabbling. She say easy easy:

"Doc, look, I have a list here. You have any of these items?"

Ole-man Beresford put on his halfa spectacles, squint-up his face, and peep at the list.

"Ohhh! Ho-ho-ho," he say. "John de Conqueror Oil? Yes, yes, I have it. And Must Oil? Yes, yes, you having *man*-worries, eh? Yes, yes, yes, let me see . . ."

And poor Clarise so shame she don't know what to do, cause ole-man Beresford calling out all the things on the list and giving advice hard hard. So hard she know people hearing and looking although she frighten to look and see is who hearing.

"Compelling Oil? Yes . . . Commanding Oil? . . . Yes . . . Ho-ho! Hmm . . . they the same, you know. Love *what*? No, no, that's call Love *Drops!* Love Drops and Stay-to-Me Oil? Yes, we have them *all,* my dear lady. Wait here, I'll fix you up. We'll see . . . The Olive Oil is for your light, right? Yes, yes, we know, we have plenty of orders for . . ."

Ow Lawd! Was *too* embarrassing for poor Clarise to bear, but she stand-up easy and wait till ole Doc come back talking all over his face bout how he know the thing cause women coming every day to buy . . .

They make a kinda speakeasy lamp with a floating wick to burn with the olive oil. The obeahwoman come to her house one morning after Harold gone to work and noint Clarise with the oils and wipe out the house talking all the time and telling her, "You must keep de lamp burning for *nine* days, all twenty-four hours in de day. Don't let it go out. And you must say Psalm Thirty-five. When you say: 'Contend O Lord with those who contend gainst me'? You must call your husband and his sweetwoman name . . . You going see," the obeah-woman tell Clarise. "In twenty-one days' time? Your life will get back good good, if not before. I ain't even going charge you. I leave it to you to give me a present. When you see your results? You *self* going come and bring me a present, then we going cook some food and go by de seawall and feed de spirits.

"But I *warn* you, you must remember to come back when you see your results, or is tumble-up your life, going tumble-up again."

Was true!

Harold get calm and tame like a lamb in just over two weeks' time. Just like Mr. Goring, he was coming home soon and staying home. Clarise carry a nice pair of gold earrings for the obeahwoman and the Saturday after that they cook one set of food and carry it by the seawall to feed the waterspirits. They meet a nice Indian family who had they own work that day. They tell Clarise that every year they doing it and they getting through nice nice with they life.

But what? After a nice two years? Harold just ups heself justso and is gone he gone off behind Leonie.

That night after that nice day at the picnic at Timehri Airport? Clarise didn't guess what waiting for her when she reach home. When the bus stop for her at the corner on the public road? She say goodnight to everybody then start to pick her way over the mud and the holes in the road, careful to look where she going before she end up in the putta-putta.

When she reach near the house she look up.

The house in darkness.

Clarise heart start to beat buddupbuddupbuddupbup! fast fast fast. Her hand cover her mouth she stop breathing and she stand-up stock still. Then she start to run, in the mud and putta-putta in the grass cross the bridge over the trench up the steps calling, "Harold? Harold? Harold?" wondering, Where Harold? Where de children? Why de house so dark?

And Miz Goring nextdoor call out, "Come, Clarise chile. They here. De children here with me."

And Clarise stop bramming down her own front door run down the steps jump over the drainer nearly fall in the gutter running upstairs to Miz Goring with her heart in her mouth . . .

"Where Harold?"

And she nearly faint when Miz Goring say, "He gone, Clarise. He gone to America this afternoon. I know how you feel. You could imagine my shock when he ask me to look de children till you come home cause he going to America. I ask him, I say, 'But how you could going to America justso and nobody don't know? Not even your wife?' "

"And what Harold say, Miz Goring?"

"He ain't pick-he-teeth, chile, he just go along his way. A car was waiting for him outside. A hirecar. Come inside and rest your feet, chile. I doanno what to tell you."

All that nice nice picnic-feeling gone. Clarise stand-up pon Miz Goring doorstep, asking herself, Is All Fools Day today or something? And is not me stand-up here at Miz Goring doormouth watching my children with they eye round and full and hearing this story here? Is another body, not Clarise Cumberbatch who just done enjoy herself at de base? Harold gone where? America? Justso? Without a word? Not even a *explanation* self?

The same afternoon while she was enjoying herself at the church outing at Timehri Airport, one of the planes taking off to America over her head was taking Harold away?

Eh-eh! Harold fool her. He fool her good! Wasn't no obeah see-far woman. Wasn't no Stay-Home-Compelling and Must-Commanding oils burning in speakeasy lamp and Thirty-fifth Psalm . . . Was tricks! Is that is what it was. Was tricks!

Leonie in America and she send for Harold. All he was doing was biding his time while he telling Clarise how he could never ever leave her. He even send in a request for her birthday on the radio station. That big-voice Pancho call it out on the air, the "Best by Request" program! "For Clarise Cumberbatch of Beter-verwagting Village on the East Coast who celebrates her birthday today. From her ever-loving-never-leaving husband, Harold." And then Pancho put on that thing like a echo so that when he call Harold name it go Haro-oro-oro-oro-orold or something so. And Harold name echoing and jerking and fading away when it call pon the air that day.

Eh-eh! All them people who come to tell Clarise they hear request come over the air for her mustbe was laughing at her behind her back? Harold even go so far as to confess that Leonie was his woman yes, but now they done, break-up, finish. He tell Clarise that life too hard in Guyana and they must try to save some money and he will try to get a visa to the States. He say he would go first then send for her and Clarence and Eunice. Harold didn't tell her he and Leonie had big plans.

But they use to talk. He say *so much* to her he can't forget? He should know she going come after him. He shouldn't be surprise to hear that she here. Cause is three years nearly done since he gone and not a word, not a line yet?

One of the last things she remember him saying is that he ain't telling nobody his plans to go to America. He say he going leave work justso and go, cause he ain't no big-shot, he don't have no big-work, so nobody ain't going pull him off airplane say he leaving before his contract up, or that he thief money, or look to cancel his passport, or something so. He too small for that. Harold only driving car for the minister of works. But he say even though the minister does treat him like a real man, he not even telling *him* his plans, cause he might convince him to stay home and then he will always have it in his mind that his chauffeur discontent and want to go to America.

And that same day Harold tell her these things, Eunice come home from small-school she use to go then:

"Mammie, you must please put another sugarcake in my lunchbox so Miss could get one. She *always* hungry."

And Miz Hercules who was paying Clarise a lil afternoon visit say that one day she didn't have not one thing to put in her chile lunchbox and the boy refuse to go to school. She say she tell him he must go to school and she will see if she could pawn a lil gold chain she have and try to scrape-up something for them to eat when he come home afternoon. But the boy cry he cry he cry. She tell him, "Boy, why you so foolish? Is not de first time you going school without breakfast to carry." "But Mammie," the boy say, "I don't want to look at no jumbie today."

And when Miz Hercules get to the bottom of the story? It seem that so much children was going school without breakfast in they lunchbox that when is time to eat, the teachers would line them up and put them to face the burial ground near the school so that they won't distress they poor lil hearts looking at they friends who eating food while they mouth only running water.

And Harold lying down on the bed inside, start to cuss:

"Is what is going on in this place, eh? Clarise, I hear they want de teachers to open de lunchbox and see if they have anything make with wheatflour inside, cause flour is a bann-item. Hell, man! I know they start to run *gestapo* pon contraban food, but why pon what de children eating?"

"No, Harold, that don't happen still. It couldn't work. It stop, Miz Hercules say."

But Harold continue cussing that day.

"And is how much wheatflour cakes and roti you going find in them lunchboxes? When men like me, not just children, eating sugarcake? *One* sugarcake! A lump of coconut-and-sugar for breakfast these days? Why you think de people calling it crisis cake? Y'think is joke? I ain't able with this, Clarise, I got to go!"

"But Harold, it ain't easy to get visa."

"I know, but I going try."

"You apply yet?"

"Yes."

"When you expect to hear?"

"Any time now."

He didn't tell Clarise that he and Leonie had the big-plans.

Steewpps! I wonder if Miz Hercules did know that day? Clarise asking herself while she take-up her position by the merry-go-round cause now she see her grip. Ow Lawd! Watch how de string bust-up. Is a good thing I put de valuables in Miz Goring canvasbag.

Well I tell you, Clarise chile? Them people mustbe properly laugh at you behind your back. All o' them who come with they sympathy when Harold gone? De same people you chase away say you don't want to hear no more story cause you and your husband living good? Ha! Girl? When they come to sympathize with you? Them mustbe was saying in they mind, *De damn fool! We try to tell her, but she won't listen.*

Tell me what? Clarise say to herself. That Leonie was Harold passage and his visa easy easy so? I had to go and slave for de American ambassador wife for nearly three years before they help me get my visa for holiday. Come to think bout it? He did tell me . . . He did tell me . . . Ow, but why he had to do it so? He couldn't bear lil more pressure?

The day after Harold pack-up the traps and go away, Miz Goring say, "Clarise chile? Is what you going do?"

"I will wait and see. He going write to me."

"But wait for what, Clarise? What use that going be, Clarise? He not going write . . . Something gone wrong. You still think —"

"Whether use or no use, Miz Goring, what I can do? I will wait and work and save and see."

"I hope you find a job, cause that is a *man* these days. But what you going waste your time waiting and hoping that man going write you from America for? Last

22

night you say you don't want him back. Now today you still hoping."

"Yes, Miz Goring, I still hoping. I have to hear from him, from Harold self. I have to wait — or go, if I don't hear nothing, before I decide bout him."

"You have to *wait* to hear from him, y'have to *go* to Harold . . . Clarise, you ain't making sense. Is how you going go, eh? You know how hard it is to get a visa? And how much is the ticket to America these days? Watch all de people every day stand-up burning-up in de hot sun pon Main Street? Is what you think they waiting for? Is visa to go to America they hoping for, and half them don't get through. Is how you going get visa, eh? And is where you going get de money from? I don't know your business, Clarise . . . These days it costing a lil fortune to go to America. De passage is over *three thousand dollars!* And too-besides? Is what you going do with your children? Especially if you get through and you going.

"Hiyah! Chile? If I was you and something like this did happen to me in this guava-season? I woulda make up my mind to band my waist and get-up-and-get, hear? Especially if I did have lil pickney like you have. You see how children punishing in this country today? Some of them when they should be in school only out in de streets hustling with two plantain chips and salted nuts, lil sweetie and mosquito coils. That's why other people who trying with they own and the small-school having such a hard time with them.

"De children these days don't want to go to school! They seeing how they friends making money robbing people in de streets and planning to turn vendor-and-trader when they grow up like they uncle and auntie who can afford to buy powdermilk for ninety dollars a tin and jump pon airplane every minute like if is *bus,* to go to America and Brazil and Surinam and Barbados to haul in de contraban."

Was good advice Miz Goring give Clarise that day. And she wag her finger in Clarise face when she say:

"Chile, you better stay home and mind your children, hear? Y'know that coolieman name Bullah? The greensman? How he always boasting bout his lil son like de boy de only chile with brains in Guyana? Well de other day I see Bullah by de sideline dam. I wanted to hide, but he see me first, and as usual he start to tell me bout de boy, Missoon. He say, 'Teacher say she na know what wrong with that boy these days, since he mother gone America? He only scratching scratching heself and he ain't know nothing no more. He cannot answer not one questions. Like he loss! All he interest in schoolwork gone. Well, Missoon mammie can't come back now till she hear bout she Permanent and then she going send for we. Me is the one who have to make sure he take in he schoolwork good here so that he going be ready for America. So what me do is me give de teacher a lil small-piece, y'know? To keep lil close to de boy. But y'see nighttime? When he crying say he want he mammie? Me does tell he, Boy! Na cry to me. Me canna help you, cause me crying too.'

"Y'see?" Miz Goring say to Clarise. "Missoon daddy have small-piece to give teacher. And evenso if you have small-piece and you find a teacher who *taking, you* can't be sure that that lil extra attention from de teacher is sufficient for your chile. You was there to hear what teacher Marje was saying that day at de meeting, how all de children who parents gone to America to send for them like they can't think bout nothing else except when they parents going get through and all they doing is

24

dreaming bout when de next barrel will come with they trackshoes and tapedeck and . . . You think is fun? Look!"

Miz Goring give one last wag of her finger at Clarise and say, "Take my stupid advice, Clarise. Forget that man! Forget America! Stay home and look after your children, hear?"

Two

Steewpps! Clarise let out a long suckteeth in Kennedy Airport.

Steewpps! Clarise suck her teeth again and start mumbling to herself now.

Eh-eh! Watch me in America? Is me Clarise in America . . . But this was not how it was suppose to be. This wasn't how me and Harold did plan it. I shoulda been here with my husband waiting at de airport cause he send for me and later we going send for de children. I wasn't suppose to come here pon my *hardness* so! But I wonder if he still going say to me is lies, is all lies. And he didn't do it cause Leonie is his woman. He do it all for me, for we. And if I did stay home and wait he woulda write me soon and he woulda send for me and de children? I wonder if he would insult me so?

I have to find that man. All these years he gone and

I *still* can't rest till we meet eyeball-to-eyeball. I ain't
come here to row. I don't want to lick-down and fight-
up with Leonie. This time I will make sure that Leonie
and me don't butt-up. But I have to find him. He have
to look me dead in my eye and tell me he was only fooling me. That he finish with the life we had together.
This is justso he going forget he have two lil children
that worship the dirt he walk pon. Eh-eh! That could
never be. No! After all, is not me only make them. And
he was a good father. Is what happen so? Pressure?

Yes, pressure. Pressure coming down pon everybody in Guyana these days. But when you call y'self a
man and you swear that man is de greatest creature
God ever make, you can't just blame everything pon de
government and run away and gone justso without a
word. If I use to complain to him bout pressure coming
down pon me in that house trying to make de two cents
he give me stretch to feed all o' we, plus buy school
uniform for five hundred dollars and lil peas to nourish
them children brain for eight dollars a pint with the
pint-measure stuff up with newspaper underneath?

Steewpps! Clarise suck her teeth again. If I use to
tell Harold all that? Is what he woulda done, eh? He
woulda got away earlier. Cause if he can't stand his own
pressure is what if he had to hear bout mine?

Clarise remembering now that all Harold use to do
when she tell him the price of things is throw back his
head and laugh like if he going mad and then start to
sing: "Ban-um, Mr. Burnham, ban-um."

But what I was to do? Run away? Justso? Abandon
my home and gone away? Leave my children? My
country? My husband? Cause pressure too much?
Without evenself a explanation self? To he or anybody?

No! No! Is not so. That man in trouble, I telling

you. He have to be in some sort of trouble or else he couldn't acting so. I know he in trouble. Is almost three years since he gone, and he ain't write one letter yet. Not *one single* letter, one *word* self . . .

"No!" Clarise say loud loud in the people airport. But she thought she say it in her mind; she didn't know she say it out loud till a woman with a wheelbarrow full of grips look round and say, "Yes?"

"No, not you, miz-lady. I not talking to you." And the woman look at her like she think Clarise crazy.

Then Clarise collect her grip from the merry-go-round. She poke in the clothes that spilling out the sides and she tie back the rope. Now all she have in her mind is passing through customs quick so she could go out in America and meet Mavis. Mavis mustbe waiting already. Thank God for Mavis Drakes. Mavis is Clarise friend. She understand what Clarise going through. She never did like Harold.

When Clarise write and tell Mavis she coming to America to search for Harold and she want somewhere to stay? Mavis write back and say that Clarise welcome to stay with her, but she not going help her to find Harold cause she not encouraging her to find him.

In another letter Clarise tell Mavis that she trying hard to forget Harold but she still love him. Mavis write back:

"Clarise, you should thank your lucky stars that you got rid of that good-for-nothing Harold Cumberbatch. But if you say you still love him, that is the cross you will have to bear alone."

And is so Clarise picking up her canvasbag from the ground and her bust-up grip from the merry-go-round and putting them pon the wheelbarrow and rolling them off to the customsman at the counter with her mind telling her over and over and over again,

Clarise chile? You tired. Y'tired, tired, tired. The
Lawd knows how you tired, Clarise.

"Anything to declare?"
"To declare? Lemme see . . . Nothing, sir. Noth-
ing. Only that it cold. It cold bad, sir. I hope my friend
Mavis bring de coat like she promise, cause I ain't ac-
custom to no coldness. I come from Guyana, y'know?"
"What's that, ma'am?"
"I say in Guyana we don't have no coldness and it
cold here. That is all I have to declare, sir. Is that it cold
here."
And a dirtyskin Portuguese boy bust-out a big-laugh
and say, "Hey! That's *dynamite,* man!"
But the customsman he not laughing at all. All
Clarise seeing is rain setting-up in his face.
He saying, "I mean, do you have any gifts? Any
plants? Alcohol? Fruits? Gold? Currency?"
"Ohhh! Oh-ho!" Clarise say. "I see . . . ha-ha ha-
ha! Y'know what I did think? I did think you asking me
what I have to declare bout de place? If I have anything
to say bout America? And I say to m'self, Well, is how
he expect me to say anything bout de place, eh? Is what
I could know? I only just come. All I know is that it
cold. It cold baaad!"
"Ma'am? Sorry, I didn't understand what you just
said."
"Oh no! You don't be sorry bout that, mister. I did
know that would happen *before* I come here, cause I
never learn to talk American. And I can't *understand*
it, either. I have to strain my ears to hear what you saying. It ain't easy, but I know I have to try. Before I come
a friend tell me that what I have to do is stand in front
de mirror and practice to talk American, and she show
me, like: *Haw aaarrre yah?* And talking in my nose like

29

a cat. But I didn't have time for all that nonsense, so I never learn to do it right. And anyway, when I hear m'self sounding so stupid? I just —"

"You're holding up the line, ma'am."

"Don't mind me," the dirtyskin Portuguese boy say. "I have all the time in the world, and I'm *enjoying* this."

The customsman cutting-up his eye pon the dirtyskin Portuguese boy.

"Ohhh! Sorry! Sorry sorry," Clarise saying, looking round at the rest of the people waiting. "Sorry, son," she say to the boy waiting in the line behind her. From behind the boy where two women just roll up she hear one long suckteeth and somebody saying:

"*Steeewwpppps!* People like them do *really* embarrass me."

"Yes, country-come-to-town."

When you see so? Them-two mustbe just come back from showing off pon people or robbing them in Guyana, Clarise say to herself. She feel like turning back and saying to them, *Hey, allyuh-two ass-holes! This here not no ordinary town, this country come to, this here is America. This na Stabroek Market Square in Georgetown that me see with these two eyes how it could confuse buckman just come out de bush. This here is Kennedy Airport in New York and I never see nothing so yet in my livelong life and when allyuh did come first? Mustbe so y'all did feel, too. Cause a just-come is a just-come whenever you done.*

But Clarise say to herself that she is a woman know time and place, so she ain't say a word to them. She just tell the boy sorry and turn back to the customsman.

"Yes, mister, lemme see what I have . . ." And if you did see what Clarise start taking out Miz Goring canvasbag . . .

Is six green mangoes: "These is for my neighbor Miz Goring daughter. She getting baby and she write home to tell her mother how her mind steady calling for green mango with salt-and-pepper and she want to make achar, too."

Is some corn-hassar wrap up in newspaper: "This is a sweet sweet fish. It nice in curry or y'could cook it in dryfood, y'know? With ground-provisions . . . metagee."

Is a plastic bottle with peppersauce.

Is another plastic bottle with the mouth seal-up with tape: "Casareep for de pepperpot. It does preserve de meat, make it last longer. All y'have to do is warm it up."

Is a bottle of XM Rum, Gold Medal: "To burn Mavis throat in all this cold weather. I hear you can't get good rum like this over here."

Is bush-pon-top-of-bush. Bush for tea, bush for medicine, purge, bush for seasoning. Is teesam, daisy, marrio-man-poke and sweetbroom. Is lemmon-grass and pear-leaf.

"Is that all?" the customsman say after he listen to Clarise telling him bout the things she spreading out pon the counter.

This time? The two women who talk bout how Clarise embarrass them? Not only embarrass now, they frighten somebody might think they like her cause they have Guyana passport like her. They give up they space in the line. They gone along to another line.

"That is all, sir," Clarise say.

The customsman breathe hard. "We'll have to take the fruit . . ." and he start to pick up the green mangoes and put them aside.

Eh-eh! Well, what is this at all? Clarise voice ringing like a bell:

31

"No, mister! No! Ow, sir! Is how you could do such a thing? What I going to tell Miz Goring? Look! She was so nice to lend me her nice canvasbag to put everything in. That poor girl! Her mind is *calling!* Mister, you is a man, *you* don't know, you could *never* know what it is to get belly and your mind steady calling calling for something you want to eat that you can't get. But *let me tell you,* sir, my mind use to call for blackpudding steady steady when I was getting Clarence. And one day? One day I walk three miles! *Five months pregnant,* just to —"

"Lady!" the customsman say sharp sharp, cutting Clarise.

But Clarise say quick quick before the man could talk, "Scuse me lil, sir, not to say I cutting you, but all I trying to say is that that poor girl baby is going to mark! Her baby is going to *mark,* mister, if she don't get these mangoes! She *expecting* them!"

"Lady, you can't bring fresh fruit or plants into the country. That's the law."

"Ohhh! Is de law? I didn't know was de law, sir. I didn't know was gainst de law."

The customsman say nothing. He take-out what he want and push aside the rest of Clarise things and then he turn his attention to the dirtyskin Portuguese boy haversack and start ransacking it like if he know what he looking for, and he sure he going find it.

"Clarise! Clarise!"

"Clarise Cumberbatch! Look me here! This side!"

Is so Clarise hearing her name calling in a daze, in a haze, cause she staring just staring with her mouth open and she thinking:

Is where they does put all these people when they go out de airport? America mustbe have plenty space. And watch how everything rush rush! How everybody hurry hurry!

Eh-eh!

Is why everybody here so hurry so? Is where they going so fast? Is everybody catching plane and all them late for it? Lawd! Mustbe *fire*? Mustbe fire make them hurry so? And watch this thing! Eh-eh! And that is not a *whiteman*? Is a whiteman, yes! And *that* is the work he doing? I never see whitepeople working laboring work before. And watch one there mopping-up de floor. Eh-eh! But what is this at all? And is where is de fire? That is what I want to know, is where de fire is.

Clarise shiver, then she remember that Mavis say she mustn't come out the airport till she bring her a coat.

"Clarise! Is me calling you. What happen to you? Like you gone deaf or something? Is me, Mavis!"

Is Mavis?

Eh-eh! Mavis dress-up high in high-heel fine-heel shoe that come back in style. Mavis have on nice nice wig and wintercoat with fur collar like what you see people wearing in the photographs in the magazines and in the pictures pon the matinee screen. Mavis have on hat with feather!

Eh-eh! Mavis look nice!

Mavis always use to look nice, but now she look like a *real* American. Mavis take off that one gold chain she use to wear round her neck day-in-day-out till she send it to talk putagee in the pawnshop. That Portuguese man Mr. Fernandes get rich off the interest Mavis pay on that chain. Cause regular regular you could mark it absent from her neck when things bad with her. Them

33

was the hand-to-mouth days before she leave Guyana. Now watch Mavis! Just look at her!

Mavis have on a nice necklace to match her earrings. Mavis look *prosperous!*

And is so Clarise stand-up watching Mavis surprise! Eh-eh! Mavis look like a *real* American!

"Take care your eye don't drop out, hear?" Mavis say to Clarise and throw the coat round her shoulder and hug Clarise tight, laughing and saying, "Clarise! Clarise chile, y'come! Clarise in New York at last!"

"Eh-eh! Mavis? Mavis is really you?"

"Yeah, Clarise, is me. But what you watching me so for? I thief your mother white fowl?"

And Clarise laugh and hug-up Mavis. And Mavis laugh and hug-up Clarise. And then they start to talk . . .

Three

CLICK!

Is a man and a woman sit down in something like a round ring facing one-another. Is words and numbers and a sound like a BEEP! and the numbers counting backward.

"Well, look, eh? Mavis, look how here you could have matinee right in your own drawingroom justso. In Guyana some people buying that thing they call video, but is who have ten thousand Guyana-dollars to buy video? Y'have to be government minister or trader to afford one of them things.

Is the letters *SOS* write-up pon a thing behind the woman back and the man talking to her slow slow and the BEEP going BIP! and the numbers slipping backward.

"HELP!"

Is the man say HELP! and the BEEP go BIP! and the number change from ten to nine and the woman say:

"Ummm . . . RESCUE!"

And the BEEP and the numbers go on bipping and changing: BIP . . . 8, BIP . . . 7, BIP . . . 6 . . . and the man say:

"AT SEA!"

And Mavis saying, "They running outa time! Is only thirty seconds they have."

And the BEEP go BIP . . . 5 and the man say again:
"AT SEA!"

And the BEEP go BIP . . . 4, BIP . . . 3, BIP . . . 2, and the woman say:

"SOS."

And the BEEP stop bipping and the numbers run out. And somebody scream: "YES! YOU ARE THE WINNER OF TWENTY-FIVE THOUSAND DOLLARS!"

The woman jump up and the man jump up and they hug-up. And she still jumping up and down like a yoyo.

And is noise. Is clapping. Is screaming. Is whistling. Is cheering and so. People running up to the circle where the man and the woman was sitting.

Eh-eh!

Is hugging-up and kissing-up and laughing-up again.

Is music playing. Is lights flashing money . . . is lights flashing $25,000 over and over and over again . . .

"Is what? Is what is de name of this picture, eh, Mavis?" Clarise ask her friend.

"Is not a picture, Clarise. Is a gameshow. See de woman there? De black one? She win *all* de money. Is

36

she win de twenty-five thousand dollars you see flashing on de screen. That why she so happy. Well, is what you want to see now? Dis one finish. You want to see a —"

"Nutting nutting nutting! I don't want to see anything! Wait! Don't turn it off! You mean to tell me, Mavis," Clarise saying with her head shaking like if she confuse, "you mean to tell me that *that* woman is a real real woman and what I see just now is not —"

"I mean to tell you, Clarise Cumberbatch," Mavis say, "that that woman you just see, she win every cent you see pon that screen."

"And is her own money? To take? To keep? For good?"

"Yes, Clarise."

"Is how much money?"

"Twenty-five thousand dollars, Clarise. And you *see* it for y'self?"

"U.S. dollars, Mavis? She win it in U.S.? You *know* is how much you can get for a U.S. dollar in Guyana these days? Up to twelve-to-one if you go pon de Corentyne, I hear. Is U.S. dollars in truth, Mavis?"

"Yes, Clarise. Is U.S. dollars."

"But why? How?"

"Well, Clarise, you see for y'self. How you could still asking me how? It's only that we tune in late. But tomorrow morning? No! Tomorrow we have to start looking for a job. Don't worry, you will see it ag —"

"Mavis! You not joking? Turn on that thing again. Lemme see!"

"It finish, Clarise. De program is only a half hour. It finish. But if you want to see something else . . ."

"Nooo no no . . . no, Mavis! Y'know who she favor?"

"Who who favor, Clarise?"

"De girl who win that money just now? She resemble Miz Abigail up de bank. You remember her? Miz Van Rossum sister. Same high forehead and thing. And she win *all* that money? Is how long it take her to win it, again?"

"Well, de whole game is a half hour, but . . . Clarise! Y'know you right? Is truth! She really favor Miz Abbie. How she? Still so peaceful and cheerful and cooking sweet sweet food?"

But Clarise ain't taking Mavis on. Like she *shot!* She stunned. She sitting down gazing in space. And Mavis like she decide to leave her alone to catch herself cause she walk away to the kitchen.

Is so people could get confuse when they see television for the first time, especially the gameshows, where they giving away all that money. You feel it easy and that it could happen to you, too.

A little later, Mavis shout out from the kitchen and tell Clarise that she going to cook her some nice chicken fricassee cause she sure Clarise not still minding fowls in Guyana and she hear how chicken too dear for people to eat steady.

"Yes, m'dear, you will eat a sumptuous meal today and surprise your stomach lil. Lemme see . . . Potato. When last y'all see a potato? Edris take her girlchile in de supermarket here, bout eight years ago when she come over to America? And de lil girl pick up a potato and say, 'Mammie, what is this thing?'

"I will make you a potato salad," Mavis say to Clarise on the couch where she leave her dreaming. Then, "Clarise? Is how much y'all paying for beef? You getting it? At what a pound?"

But no answer.

"Talk hard, Clarise. You know I was always harda hearing. Is how de beef going?"

But all Mavis hearing is Clarise mumbling mumbling. So she leave the kitchen and walk back to the drawingroom to hear what her friend saying. And guess what she hear?

"Twelve noughts are nought, twelve noughts are . . . twelve fives are six . . . *Three hundred thousand dollars!*"

Eh-eh! Is count she counting the twenty-five thousand dollars in Guyanese?

"Ow Lawd!" Mavis groaning. "Clarise, is not so! It ain't so easy at all at all at all! We don't count so here. I know at home y'all don't go to de bank but to de market with de U.S. dollars. But here in de States we does have to go to de bank. And you not going win no twenty-five thousand dollars either, cause *that* kind of luck don't happen to everybody so. And evenso, if you win it, say? When they finish with de tax and de this-and-that? You going be working division and subtraction instead of multiplication.

"But de most important thing, Clarise, de *very first* thing you have to understand bout this place here? Is that everything you see on that TV screen is not how it going happening in your life in America. That there is 'Nancy-story,' hear? Don't you believe it!

"Aaaoow, but come, sweetheart! Don't look so like pity-pity-po'-boy-sorry-f'me," Mavis say, hugging-up her friend and pulling her up from the couch. "I will even listen to your talk bout that *cross* Harold and we will see what we can do. But later, next week or so. I giving you my whole week-leave. First you have to find a job . . . But now we going cook and eat something. Come, Clarise, come. Cheer up, man."

39

Mavis leading Clarise like a child into the kitchen cause Clarise can't catch herself yet. She thinking, Like is true what they say bout America? That this place have plenty money for everybody? In truth! Eh-eh!

"Come, man, Clarise man, don't make-up your face so! When my fellow come later on I want to show him that I have *nice* friends from Guyana like me. Come in de kitchen and keep me company while I cooking. What you want to eat? Call *anything*. I was going cook chicken and . . . but whatever you want we will cook. If we don't have it in de house we will leave and go to de supermarket on de corner and get it. Anything your mind give you to eat, just call it. Talk."

"You have any rice, Mavis?"

"Yes, Clarise, but *rice*? Ow, man! You come till here to America to eat rice? Is what wrong with you at all?"

That was Monday morning. And whole day Monday Clarise mind can't settle. All she seeing is the girl resemble Miz Abbie jumping up and laughing and all that money flashing pon the TV screen.

By nighttime when Mr. Blades come (is so Mavis boyfriend name) Clarise still counting how she would spend the money if she win it.

"But you ain't going win no money, Clarise. *You* could answer them questions?"

"Wait, Mavis, soon as I find Harold, and I learn this place lil? I going answer any question that they want me to answer for twenty-five thousand dollars."

"And is how you going get on that program in de first place? You think that so easy too?"

"I will ask —"

"And is how much more people not asking to get on it just like you and not even getting through? Look, Clarise, easy de pressure lil, ease me, hear? Is whole

day you pon de same subject. Suppose you win it . . .
What you will do?"

"Say thanks and get on a airplane with it, me and
Harold."

"And go back where? There? To *that place?*"

"What happen to *that place,* Mavis? Is home. This
place got me feeling like a fish-outa-water already. Guyana is a sweet sweet place, it only lil confuse now. But
wait! It will catch itself. Mavis, you must remember,
you must *always* remember what de ole people say, hear?
'Cuss where you go, na where you come out'!"

"Yes, Clarise, but de ole people say too, *'If heaven
is only for po' people, me na want to go there,'* " Mavis
say. Then the doorbell ring and Mavis jump up ringing
her fingers saying:

"Is Mr. Blades is Mr. Blades is Mr. Blades! *Steewpps!*
Y'know something? Is every night that man coming here,
y'know? And is what he want? A piece! *Every* night a
piece! I ain't able to have no man living in my drawers
so. Good Lawd, man! He ain't got no discretion. I too
glad you come to get he off my belly."

Mavis get up and start to giggle and shake herself
and Clarise left so watching her with her mouth open
to say something but Mavis say quick quick:

"Clarise, Clarise, listen . . ."

The doorbell ring again.

"Shush! I might don't answer and let it ring."

"But he will know that —"

"Never!" Mavis say. "Only de TV. He know that
sometimes I go out and leave it on. Chile, in this country? You could hide from your man, your bill collector,
your *mother* — anybody. Just don't answer de phone or
de doorbell. Nobody don't have no window to peep
through and see you. Sometimes you can peep . . . so."

Mavis walk over to the door and lift up a lil lid over a round glass. "Through this peephole? You can watch them and they ain't even know you here. And even if self they know? *You* don't care."

The doorbell ring again.

"Ahhh, Mavis, let de man in. If you don't want him, send him bout his business and done, but don't —"

"Send he bout he who? Girl! That man got de *living* thing, hear? Piesah! Plenty plenty money. Gapples! like Mr. Bailey use to say. Me? Send he bout he who? He business? My job can't mind me in de style I get accustom to. But I glad you come now. You going be my pussy-watchman fo —"

"Eh-eh! Me? No, Mavis! No! Never! Mavis, you gone mad or what?"

But Mavis only laughing and running to the door and opening it and smiling sweet sweet and saying, "Eh! Darling, y'come? Y'were ringing long? We were in de kitchen, we didn't hear de bell. Come in, come in! Come in and meet my friend Clarise, from Guyana. Clarise? This is my boyfriend, Mr. Blades."

Boyfriend? He don't look like no boy to me, Clarise say to herself. He look like a ole man. Eh-eh! Is how Mavis say this man living pon her belly every night? De poor man going kill heself. She better discourage him in truth. Eh-eh! Mr. Blades mustbe over sixty years! But he look like a *gentleman*. He tall and he have on a nice parson-gray suit with pinstripe and a dark red tie. He look like one of them ole-time dressmen.

Wallah wallay! Like de ole people say: *"Man a-courting must go gay,"* yeah!

Mr. Blades have all the hair on his head but it curly curly like he mix-up with somebody else and most of the gray at his temples. Since Clarise see Mr. Blades, her mind take him and she feel sorry for him cause he in Mavis hands, cause Mavis ain't no true member. Mavis going eat out every cent he have, then loose he wild.

Mr. Blades say, "So *you're* Clarise. Heard a lot about you. How *are* ya!" and he move inside the door with his hand stretch out, talking softly softly like learnedman. Is dunceman does make noise.

Clarise want to tell Mr. Blades that she hear a lot bout him, too, but she say to herself she better not do that, before he ask is what she hear.

"I all right, sir, how you?"

"Call me Curleigh. All my friends call me Curleigh."

Clarise look at Mavis thinking, But Mavis don't call him so? Mavis does call Mr. Blades Mr. Blades.

And Mr. Blades mustbe read her mind, because he laugh and say, "Oh! Mavis? She's not my friend. I've been trying for over a year now to make her my friend, but Mavis ain't easy. Are all Guyanese women so hard on a man?"

But before Clarise could answer Mavis say, "Your friend is your friend. Your husband or your man is y'husband or y'man. That is a different thing altogether."

But Clarise say in her mind, No no no. No! Mavis, no, if your husband or your man ain't your friend, is what it mean? It don't mean a thing.

"Look, y'see Harold?" she say out loud.

"Ohhh God!" Is Mavis groaning so. But Mr. Blades turn to Clarise:

"Who is Harold? Oh, yes! Your husband. Yes. Mavis, please let the woman speak, will you? Go on, tell me about Harold, Clarise. You must love him very much to come such a great distance to find him. At least I've heard from Mavis that you've come in love?"

"Ohhh, yes yes yes, Mr. Blades —"

"Call me Curleigh."

"Yes, Mr. . . . oh, Curleigh Mr. Blades. Always in love. I don't care what is his reasons, cause I know de *main* one he behaving like this. I know what . . ."

Clarise stop talking and draw in a deep breath, then she say:

"Mr. Curleigh? Is how I can describe it to you? It looking like Harold behaving irresponsible, but I know is this man-thing that driving him. It does drive y'all to do all kinds of irresponsible things so y'all could get closer to what y'all feel you have to do to take care of your responsibilities. Am I making sense, sir? I don't even know what I saying . . ." Clarise shut her mouth.

"No, no, please go on. You're making *eminent* sense, Clarise, don't stop, please."

"She *must* make sense to you, cause she always taking-up for men," Mavis say.

"I not taking-up for men, Mavis. I just trying to understand how I get left in this condition, without my man, in America, with my children left motherless and fatherless and running wild and giving they grand-mother water under her heart, I'm sure. I just want to know all all all all how I get so. That's why I want to find out what going on in Harold mind."

I use to think I did know, Clarise say to herself now, cause Mavis and Mr. Blades got they own discussion going now bout man and woman and what they should be to one-another. I use to think bout Harold as a friend and I always thought that he know he had a friend in me.

So why he don't even write, eh? What he do he done do. But just write, tell me, just write and explain. That's why I say de man mustbe in trouble. He have to be in trouble or he would never act de way he acting.

Okay, evenself you say he run away with Leonie and didn't tell you, cause naturally he couldn't tell you a thing like that straight out . . . But he used to hint hint . . . Clarise throw her mind back. Yes, he used to give you some hints, come to think bout it! Yes yes yes!

Lawd!

"Stop it, man!" Mavis say to Mr. Blades. "Got manners! Y'ain't see somebody in de house?"

Ohhh Lawd! While Clarise mind wander away, they gone inside, and like Mavis wasn't joking bout Mr. Blades.

Now de man come for his lil thing, and watch you, Clarise, in de way. And Mavis like she really mean to make you a pussy-watchman in truth. But not me! Clarise say to herself. Every night I will find a reason to leave this place when that man come to visit. Lemme start now!

"Allyuh? I going for a walk lil, hear?"

"Don't get lost," Mr. Blades say.

"No! Clarise, you don't know —" Mavis start to say, but Clarise cut her:

"I only going down de corner. I won't get loss." And she walk out and slam the door:

BLADAM!

Four

Tuesday morning before bird-wife wake. Clarise wake up with her eyes shut expecting to hear the kiskadee in the bread-and-cheese tree and Cheddi calabash knocking gainst the bucket with the water splashing while he bathing his skin at the stand-pipe in the backyard.

And neighbor Nestor baby crying and Gopaul jackass braying and the harness jingle-jangling and a fowlcock crowing and a cartwheel rolling over the dirtroad. The parrots chirping in the coconut-tree, the dogs down the road barking and bell-voice Rose running her cows to pasture. Six- and seven-o'clock workers passing with they bicycle bells ringing and the Moulvi in the mosque hollering and Miz Goring warning her husband not to go in the Russian hirecar. "That wildman going *kill* somebody one of these days!"

46

And is slow slow so Clarise waking up and realizing that she not still in Beterverwagting. And she knowing that if she open the window she not going see no sun coming up behind the fishermen coming in from the sea to the seawall by the Koker dam in they sailboats with the sweet morning dew in they face.

Clarise know she not going see them hanging they nets pon the bramble to dry, then packing the fineshrimps and coarse-shrimps, bangamary and butterfish and gilbakker and cacabelly in the big marketbaskets that they begging for a lift for the weight pon they head to begin the big-race to the marketplace.

Up the seawall down the seawall cross cowpasture to the public-road pass the funeral parlor with they hands balancing the weight pon they head . . . bodies raising up and coming down raising up and coming down . . . up and down and in and out . . . through cows and lorries and donkeycart and bicycle and East Coast bus and hirecar till they reach the Middlewalk dam and all the way to the women waiting in the noise in the market.

Clarise know already that she can't put her head out the window cause it cold like dognose outside, and even if she could look outside all she going see is a lot of square buildings, not even a backyard with grass self or a frontstep a bottom house or a bridge over a trench with some mud.

She going see a whole set of skeleton-trees with no leaves. She going have to search for the sky cause so much concrete in the way.

All she hearing is:
Crashbambraddabambam!
Baddangbang . . . BRAP!
Wheeeeyooooouuuuuu!

47

Is what?
Is traffic-noise!
Is police-car-siren-ambulance-scream!
Is somebody bawling:
Murda!
Is I and I are criminal . . . Murda!
Look, Clarise, wake up, hear? That is a Rasta-song
you hearing in your mind. You not home in Guyana.
You here in America. Here in New York . . .
"Murder!"
Is somebody outside . . .
"Murder!"
Is trailer-truck and subway-train and . . .
Rain?
Rain pon top of snow?
No!
Is what that does turn to . . . ?
But hear Mavis! Mavis in the kitchen and Clarise
can smell bacon cooking and she tell herself that she
can't even remember when last she smell it, much less
eat it.
Mavis sounding happy. Mavis singing:

" . . . ohhhhh
Fore-day-mawning cock a-crow,
hear Auntie Bess a-holla,
heist you bundle lehwe go,
hear Auntie Bess a-holla.
I feel I feel I feel I feel
I feel like a mawning-star,
I feel I feel I feel I feel
I feel like a mawning-star!
Ohhhhh!
What she holla what she holla

48

Wha' she holla fo'?
Ohhhhh . . ."

"What she holler for? . . . Clarise! It's time to get up, is time-to-get-up. Is . . . TIME!"

And is so Clarise get the courage to drag herself out of bed (a stretch-out couch in Mavis drawingroom) to go pon the road that first day she was to go out and look for work in New York. Mavis take a week out her leave to show Clarise the place.

That Tuesday morning, before they even set foot out the house, Mavis put Clarise to sit down and give her a long lecture on headhunters:

"A headhunter is somebody who would hear that you just come and would lay wait you and play like if they know you, if y'all come from the same country. Or if they can't play like they know you? They would offer you a lil advice . . . where you could go to get your pigtail or casareep or coconut and hassar in New York. And when they get you to trust them? You bound to tell them where you working or where you living, and easy so is all your business they knowing before they sell you to immigration."

"Headhunters!"

"Is so some people calling them, but I does call them chickenhawk! Cause is same way them chickenhawk swooping down sudden sudden and picking off people fowls? Is so them headhunters catching people like you unawares in New York, Clarise. People say all that stop, but I say, Once-a-chickenhawk-always-a-chicken-hawk!"

Mavis tell Clarise that even after she, Mavis, come into status and get her Permanent she still looking for chickenhawk in New York cause she get so accustom to doing it. That's why she feel she know every last one of them who preying pon Guyanese.

"And de kingpin is Mr. Andrew Grimes. He does prey pon everybody, not only Guyanese."

Before she take Clarise pon the road that day, Mavis tell her how she could suss-out chickenhawk in New York.

"You could know them by they looks, how they hovering bout de place like they waiting for something or they looking for you. Know how sometimes you could watch a person and tell that person up-to-tricks? Well is so . . . The thing to do is don't talk to strangers in New York. Cause sometimes they face would look knowing, cause a chickenhawk could come from de village nextdoor yours and you don't know he, or *she,* too! Remember, Clarise, *woman na gentleman* in this here Babylon-town here, hear? After all, *you na thief till you get catch,* right?

"Watch out for de *knowing* faces. Always try to see them before they see you. If you see them first? Bend down, tie your shoelace, duck in a store, or just run like hell. *Don't let them catch up with you!* That's all — don't let them catch up with you!

"If you on a train? Get off at de wrong stop. Turn back or walk up, but make sure they not following you. If you let them catch up with you? De next thing you know is Guyana Airways going be announcing it departure from Kennedy Airport to Timehri and is you pon that plane going home dry dry so before you evenself get a chance to *pee* in New York City. Y'know? And that mean is deport . . . y'get deport . . .

"BLADAM! Justso."

• • •

And that was a week! When it end? Mavis swear to Clarise that she not doing it again for *anybody*. Not even if her mother was to come out the grave and ask for help so. Cause Clarise lead her a *dance* whole livelong week.

But Mavis is another-one. What she expect going happen when you take a Guyana countrygirl out the country in Guyana and drop her deep in the heart of New York near Forty-second Street and Broadway there?

Eh-eh! First thing Mavis do is she take that poor countrygirl from Beterverwagting who ain't quite recover yet from the airplane she come in and from seeing all them jets setting down and taking off from all them airports she pass through, and Mavis dragging her on a *escalator* to the subway.

Eh-eh!

"Look, Mavis! Is what is this thing? Step ain't suppose to walk along with you so? Step suppose to stand-up one place while you walking. At de airport I nearly fall down and bust m'head on one of these things, hear? Mavis! Take care I fall down, hear?"

"No, Clarise. You not going fall down. Give me your hand. Now! Step on so! Oopps! See? It easy."

"Yes, I see, is easy . . . But I don't know where we going. Is why we going down in de earth so? Is where we going, eh? To visit Beelzebub? If you was to start entering de earth in Guyana so you know how much Dutch jumbie you would disturb?"

"Is de trains down here, Clarise."

"In de earth so? In de ground? Y'all don't feel funny coming down here so? Y'all don't frighten? And suppose they was to have a earthquake?"

"New York don't have earthquake, Clarise."

"Okay, Mavis, all right. Not say I botheration . . .

But as f'me? You must please show me de busway above de ground, hear?"

"You could get in a accident pon de bus, too, Clarise."

"Yes, I know that, Mavis. Life is a whole big-accident I could get into every single day after day after day. But I always want to see de sky above my head, cause my grandmother tell me stories her grandmother tell her bout how she come from Africa in de ship . . .

"Mavis? People don't *talk* to one-another here?"

"Not if they don't know one-another, Clarise."

"Watch all this smoke coming out my mouth, Mavis."

"Is de cold, Clarise, is de cold make so."

"Mavis? Is why this place so dirty so? Why it have so much rubbish rubbish rubbish all over?"

"I don't know, Clarise. And Clarise! Clarise, please! Stop staring-down people so!"

"Ayeayeayeayeaye! Watch, Mavis! Look at that lady there! She is a real mashereen, eh? And watch that stasher by her side! Ain't he favor Elroy? Remember? That lil nakedskin boy his mother run away in de gold bush with a pork-knocker and leave his father to mind him? He turn out *nice*, though. If I ain't mistaken I believe he right here in America studying doctor. Watch, Mavis man, see if that man don't resemble Elroy!"

"Clarise, I not watching *nothing*, cause you going get us in plenty plenty story pon this road today. This is not *Guyana*, Clarise, this is *New York!* You can't bring your *fastness* here. Look! Watch round you . . . see if you see anybody staring-down people and pointing so? You could get y'self in big-big-story so, y'know? In this country you does have to try to settle y'self quick-time,

Clarise, cause you ain't see nothing yet in New York and if you start off like this? You will soon giddy.

"And y'can't bring no Guyana-fastness here, either. Over here curiosity does *really* kill de cat, hear? I can't stop you from staring, Clarise, but don't do it so open . . . And f'Godsake, Clarise, don't point! Don't point! Pleeease! Don't point . . ."

Is so Mavis have to be going steady steady:

"Ow, Clarise, Clarise, come along, now, eh? Clarise, people could get they dead for less than that in this place here, hear? . . . Clarise, come along, Clarise! For de last time I telling you, and I not going tell you again! Clarise, you're not home in Guyana. This is not Guyana, Clarise. This is America! Stop talking to strangers pon de road! And don't *point,* Clarise. Please try not to point!"

Clarise in Wonderland!

Her mouth open. Her eye like cookshop-fly, no sooner lighting pon something than darting off to something else:

Is two young people hugging-up and kissing-up long long long.

"In de big-broad-public daylight so? Lawd!"

Is a man dress-up in woman clothes and he walking and flouncing-up heself like *Tell-Marie-not-to-marry-to-Jacob-all-cause-he-does-walk-and-shake-up!*

"Mavis! Mavis, look look look what is that? Is a he or a her? Or . . . eh-eh! But look this *story!* Is a boy! Mavis, is a *boy!* Aaooww! Lawd? But he make a *nice* girl, eh? Lawd-Jesus? Come for your world!"

This time Mavis gone, mumbling to herself while she hustling out of there, "God-Lawd! Is cuss going happen right-away now or somebody going take out a gun and —"

"CLAR-ISE!"

Mavis run back quick quick and take her friend hand and is so she dragging Clarise away begging the man dress-up in woman clothes pardon:

"Don't worry with her, miss . . . er . . . I mean mist . . . er. You see, she just-come-from-away . . . from de country, and —"

"Well, what're *you* so upset about, bitch? All she did was pay me a *com*pliment!"

Was a big-story so every day!

Clarise only talking talking to strangers on the bus in New York like if she on the Scheme bus or the Ruim-veldt or Linden bus at home. But even home people stop talking talking pon the bus. They too burden down with the worries and the troubles. They staring in space and not saying a word to one-another. Just like here in America. People just staring at nothing.

All the same, Mavis manage to prapra Clarise, push her, hunch her, drag her, coax her, beg-and-beseech her, cuss her, and threaten to be done-with-she, till they get through with all the places she want to cover Tuesday and Wednesday. But it wasn't easy at all.

Tuesday morning the first agency they go to is on Thirty-seventh Street, for Household Help. Place crowded. As soon as they walk in the door, Clarise spot somebody she know and she start off:

"Eh-eh! Maizel! Is you? Is what you doing here?"

But the Maizel-woman she talk to playing like she don't know Clarise or she don't hear her call her off or something. She only looking away and Mavis notice two more women sitting in the corner pulling up the magazines they reading in front they face.

"Like Maizel don't hear me," Clarise say.

"Yes, she hear you, she hear you she hear you,

Clarise. But is quaintance she don't want to make quaintance with you here. Ress-up, ress-up. Rest up!"

"Eh-eh! But watch Babsy, too . . . and . . . like is *everybody* here today?"

Quick-time! Mavis drag Clarise through the door.

"Why? Is why you do that, Mavis?"

"Cause you too hard-ears, Clarise. Y'must learn to hear! Them people in that place don't want to know you now. They have problems. They mustbe don't even have they greencard and you going expose them easy easy so."

"What I would do a thing like that for? I —"

"Don't worry with that now, Clarise. Just come. And remember what I tell you this morning, that's all."

And Wednesday night? Is Mavis sprawl-off pon her bed groaning:

"Boneweary! Boneweary! I am bone weary! Clarise, for de past two days, day-in day-out, is me and you drilling round New York trying to find a job for you, till when de nighttime come I can't wait to throw my calico body down pon de bed and close my eyes and go to sleep. But like tonight de sleep won't come, Clarise. Too tired. So tired I don't even want to watch 'De Jeffersons.' So tired that if I hear Harold Cumberbatch name call *one more time,* I will throw your ass outside in de cold, friend or no friend."

"Okay, Mavis. Okay. But what happen? You don't want to talk at all or is just Harold Cumberbatch name you don't want to hear?"

"No, talk talk talk, Clarise. Tell me bout home . . ."

And is so de ganga go:

"How Hilda? How Abbie? How Gigi? Uncle Oscar getting better? M.C. get my letter? And what bout Van? I hear he turn big-propertyman!"

55

"Dudley gone to Surinam and Allan and he wife left. And chile, your country in a state . . . Wait! You only *think* you know story. Wait till you *hear* . . . People does have to wait sometimes for months-at-a-time to get lil fry-oil, soap, salt. We have to cook pon coalpot, *that* is we lot. We have to line-up for this, line-up f'that . . . And y'see butter? Milk? Cheese?

"Jeez!

"De people who vending-and-trading? Is them who making a living. Some of them who was po'-ass just like me? Is them who now dishing-it-up. Plane turn like bus these days. Is everybody hauling in de goods and calling on de prices. De government say is de *parallel economy* but all o' we know is de *only* economy.

"When de government start seizing de cars that fetching de flour? De traders start using de funeral parlor. Don't laugh, Mavis, is true story I telling you. I hear a funeral parlor hearse was busy busy busy between Corentyne River and de city. De police stop them at de tollgate.

"Wait! Hear! Listen!

"You think was corpse wrap up in tarpaulin in them coffin? No, m'dear, was flour they fetching!"

"And what bout that Jonestown story?"

"That Jonestown story? Chile, it stink-up de place, was a *living disgrace!* And too-besides? It change-up de price of American dollars. Too much Jonestown money in de streets. That was when people stop going de bank and start banking in de market.

"Remember Cheap Street? That turn Vendor's Arcade! That Jonestown story? . . .

"And pon top of *that*? Guess what! They kill Miz Rodney son. Yes, justso . . . Boom! Walter gone!

"But, Mavis? Them say is not truth say Walter

Rodney dead, cause people does hear him talking pon de mall. Some say they even see him in de market. And is not everybody born with caul . . ."

And when Mavis think Clarise fall asleep she only hearing:

"Mavis! Mavis, what is that thing over there?"

"Is what is what, Clarise?"

"That thing over there."

"Clarise, what *thing* over . . . Look! Clarise? Don't bring no Guyana jumbie here, hear? What thing over whe — Ohhh! I now see what you talking bout. Hah! Y'damn fool! Is de shadow of de TV pon de wall. See? De television over there and de . . . You best go to sleep now, Clarise. Like you getting bassidy or something. Like Harold Cumberbatch have your head bassidy."

"Is Harold or New York, Mavis?"

"Whatever . . . go to sleep, Clarise. *Goodnight,* Clarise!"

"Goodnight, Mavis . . .

"Eh-eh, Mavis?"

"Ow, Clarise, sleep, nuh? You haunted? Is what now, eh?"

"Mr. Blades ain't come tonight?"

"Y'see not, chile? Your C-clerking like it working."

"Mavis, don't say that, please. Every living night that man come I finding myself in de drugstore or de supermarket at de corner, drinking coffee or examining de prices pon de goods. Thing good over here, eh? Y'see a tube of toothpaste in Guyana? Y'know how much for it on de pavement?"

"Sleep, Clarise. God! Sleep sleep sleep! Tomorrow is another day of it . . ."

Five

Thursday morning, the morning before the last day of Mavis leave. Clarise wake up praying, walking shivering with cold to the bathroom. Mavis say is better to sleep under plenty blankets than to sleep with heat. Is true. But when time come to get from under the blanket? That is the story. In the middle of the night when you want to pee and you tell yourself you going to hold that water till morning come but you feeling uncomfortable and the sleep not sweet no more? You have to get up and go . . .

And now Clarise walking to the bathroom, standing-up there staring her face in the mirror with all the boo-boo in her eye and her hair cass-cass and Clarise saying, praying:

Dear God, you who is *the lifter of my head*. Let this cup pass from me. Let it, please? A job, some money, and strength enough to carry on, dear God, that is all I ask. I know he out there and he catching more hell than me, cause he never been there like me. And I would always come through with your help.

Clarise wipe the boo-boo from her eye. "Help me, Lawd!"

That day they try four places in all. One advertisement say under "Help Wanted, Domestic": "Mature woman wanted to take charge of household. In Queens." Mavis tell Clarise she not going get the job. Clarise ask her why? And she is a mature woman? And she take care of her household for sixteen years since she marry to Harold? But Mavis say:

"Clarise, I give up this whole week for you, so nothing I do is going waste my time. Is yours, and you have to learn. Let us go to Queens. But first we have to call and say we coming. And remember what you been forgetting *all* week: don't *talk* too much, Clarise.

"Your name is Mavis Drakes and I name Clarise. Look, take this. This is your greencard. And de hairdo I give you this morning is exactly de one I wearing in de picture. Only you won't straighten de damn nigger-knots pon your head lil bit. But nobody won't notice, don't worry. *They* think we all favor one-another. They not going notice a *thing*. Don't worry."

Was a long long train drive. Stop after stop after stop. Mavis like she drop asleep and she now come back to meet Clarise in deep deep conversation with the man sitting down next to her. Eh-eh! Watch Clarise, eh? Just *watch* her! Is how she get so far so fast? And watch the surprise on Mavis face . . .

". . . but me and Harold, we never go in balcony. First of all we couldn't afford it. We does go in pit. We is pittites. And y'see when is a war-picture or a cowboy?

59

With fighting-up and killing-up and so? Y'know? Is justso I would find m'self left so, watching Harold and de other men in de theater giving-and-taking de blows even-and-straight with John Wayne and what's-his-name . . . not Sydney Poitier — everybody like him, too, but not for fighting-up and killing-up pictures. Is de other one I mean . . . Wait, lemme ask Mavis." Clarise make to turn to Mavis, then she remember: "Jim Brown! Is him!"

"Clarise, is when last you been to a picture, eh? Jim Brown gone out long . . . and John Wayne *dead*." Mavis hunch Clarise in her ribs and then she shake her shoulder like if she catch herself and she decide that she not getting involved in no foolishness . . .

But it have to stop!

"Clarise!"

"Just a second, Mavis, lemme finish telling my friend this story . . ."

"Friend? Friend? Is how you find friend so fast? Well this is some *real* Guyana-strokes you pulling here." And now Mavis peeping round Clarise to see this *friend* Clarise talking bout.

Eh-eh!

Is a cleanface young man sitting down near Clarise with a look on his face as if he saying to heself, "Why me, O Lord, why me?" And guess what he have in his hand.

Eh-eh!

Mavis open her eyes wide and she crane her neck like if she trying to see if is truth what she seeing, or if she seeing doubles.

But is truth! The cleanface young man have a picture of Harold Cumberbatch in his hand.

"Lawd! What is this?" Mavis say.

And Miz Clarise still carrying on at a rate:

". . . and is so they giving-and-taking de blows: hmmm ugh! baddap! whaddap! buddupp! Dish-it-in-he-skin! Ouch! Man? You cruel, y'know? You win y'win y'win! No! Not yet! Bop! Ohhh! Nooooo!"

Eh-eh? Is so Clarise have Mavis and a whole trainful of people watching her. And Clarise still carrying on like the pittites in the cinema in Guyana.

". . . Braddap-bap! Ouch! Make him pay for that. Yeah! Look, man, dish-it-in-he-skin. Y'see! Y'see! He loss that grin. Waxen! Blaxen! Caxen! Budduppbap!"

"Clarise, STOP!"

Clarise breathing hard. "Okay, Mavis, just now. Wait a lil till I finish telling this boy this thing . . ."

"Clarise!"

Mavis hunch Clarise in her ribs again.

"Mavis, stop, man, you tickling me."

Mavis say, "Ow God! Help me, *please*? This woman, this woman . . . ?" Mavis pinch Clarise hand hard and twist her flesh.

"Clarise, you *can't* do that. People don't call men *boy* in America. They does vex! And too-besides, Clarise, look how everybody on de train watching. You come here to perform? I sure some people getting off before they reach they stop cause they think there is a mad-woman here."

"Ow, Mavis, give me a lil chance to finish my story. I promise I will stop just now . . ." And she look round at the people on the train.

But nobody not noticing. "Mavis, watch . . . everybody minding they own business. Is only you digging. Don't-*dig*, Mavis, don't dig. Wait!"

But Mavis say people only *playing* they not noticing Clarise.

"Don't tell *me,* Clarise. I *live* in this place. You just come. They think you *mad,* Clarise. They *frighten,* that's why they won't look at you. They frighten you going turn on them. You ain't even notice how much of them get away already? Ow, Clarise, stop now, eh?"

"Okay, Mavis, one second more . . ."

"And don't *talk* bout a Muhammad Ali fight. Look, mister? One night I watch my husband trade blow-for-blow when Muhammad was fighting. He wasn't even *seeing* de fight, he was listening it on de radio. And y'see when that fight was over? My husband drop down pon de bed and he say, 'Whew! Clarise? That was a *hard* fight, girl. That fight was hard bad.' "

Mavis sit back and relax like she think Clarise done. But Clarise turning back to the cleanface young man:

"Mister? I may never get another chance to re-member to ask a man this question that I have pon my mind, so lemme ask you now. Mister, is why y'all stay so, eh? Is why men stay so? Is cause somebody draw somebody with de world pon they back and show y'all? Is cause de drawing have a man face pon it?"

"Ow Lord!" Mavis say, and she look like she give up now. She peeping round Clarise again to see how the young man taking that one.

Eh-eh! The young man smiling? The train pulling into the Utica Avenue station. He get up. Is his stop.

"Praise Christ!" Mavis say under her breath again when she see the young man get up to leave, but the man hear her. He look at Mavis hard. He say to Clarise:

"I have to get off here, sister, but I really would like to talk to you again . . ."

"No!" Mavis holler quick quick before Clarise could open her mouth to answer. "This Clarise? This woman? She won't *hear!* She won't *learn!* Like she going have to *feel* first!"

The young man look at Mavis again before he say to Clarise:

"Okay, sister. Your friend's right. You shouldn't be talking to strange men on trains. But I'm glad you spoke to me. You're a *dynamite lady*. If I see Harold, I'll tell him . . ."

The young man show Clarise a cuff, and he gone.

"Clarise, is how much of them pictures of Harold Cumberbatch you have, eh?"

And Mavis eye open wide when Clarise open her purse and take out a big-bundle so! Harold pictures! Poor Mavis like she shot! She can't believe her eyes.

"Is where you get all them pictures of Harold Cumberbatch from, Clarise?"

"When I been in de drugstore de other night? I see a sign say, 'Special on Family Photos — Send to Friends and Relations.' This is a special on Harold photo that I bring from Guyana. I collect them last night."

"Is how much of them, Clarise?"

"Is only a hundred. When I work and get pay every week I will take out another hundred. Even if is not special I think I could afford it. This cost twenty dollars."

"TWENTY DOLL — *Clarise!* You gone mad or what?"

"Mustbe, Mavis. But I still know what I doing. So don't try to stop me. You're a good friend to me. Nobody else I know woulda take me in like you and put up with all this foolishness . . ."

Clarise stop talking, but something else on her mind and Mavis waiting to hear, like if she know her friend is not a woman to take-she-stomach-make-bankhouse.

At last Clarise start to talk again:

"But Mavis, you and me we going have to make up our mind if we going part company now and stay friends, cause I not going stop trying to find Harold till I find him and I know you never going get to like Harold Cumberbatch."

Clarise pause again, then she say:

"Mavis, you is my friend. Don't vex with me for asking . . . but, you *like* men? I don't think you like men. No no no, Mavis, I don't mean to say what you thinking, I just want to know if you *like* men, like how you would like a pet dawg, or cat even."

Mavis say, "Ow Lawd!" and she looking like she want to say something but she don't know what to say. Like she irritate but she don't know why.

And then like Mavis forget Clarise is waiting for a answer and she have a look on her face like if she answering the question for herself in her mind. Clarise know all that her friend pass through with men, from her stepfather who use to have sex with her in the latrine, to all the boys and men who lie they head off to her till she come to never believe a *sinful word* that drop from the lips of men. Clarise was Mavis friend for long and she know, cause Mavis tell her.

"Like all I want to do now is use them. Take they money and de lil sex when my mind call. No, I don't like men," Mavis say. But it looking like she thought she say it in her mind, like she don't know she say it hard. Cause when she see Clarise looking at her with a I-did-know-it look pon her face? Mavis say quick quick:

"But I don't like women, either!"

"Well that is you, Mavis. I *love* women," Clarise say.

64

Six

Mavis was right. They didn't get the job for Clarise. How Clarise going get the job when she forget is she name Mavis cause is Mavis greencard she using?

"Yes, Mavis, tell me about yourself," the lady say after she come to the door herself (and holding the big-ferocious dog looking like the one does guard Munni-man rumshop in the village back home) cause she say she don't have nobody to answer the door and take care of business and that is what she advertise for a person for.

Is that-monster-that I will have to hold back from people? Clarise asking herself, eyeing-off the dog what cutting-up his eye pon them and straining in his collar.

The lady who advertise for the job is a nice woman. She have a face like the moon smiling over the garden wall in the poem Clarise use to say when she was at school. She have on hardpants and a fullblouse paint-up all over. She is a artist, she say, work downstairs in her basement. She want somebody to take care of the house cause things falling apart, she say, and she can't do it herself because it taking up too much of her time. And they, Mavis and Clarise, look like two capable enough women and:

"Which one of you is Mavis? Mavis Drakes?"

Yes, she have a face like de-moon-has-a-face-like-a-clock-in-de-wall. It shines . . . smiles . . . *Steewpps!* Is true what Sparrow say in that calypso: "If my mind was brilliant I woulda been a damn fool. Cause is all this stupid stupidness they teach me in school." Cuthridge was *really* trying to keep us in ignorance in truth with them schoolbooks he write for us: "And Dan is de *man* in de van . . ." "Mr. *Mike* goes to school on a bike . . ." "Twurley and Twisty were two screws . . ."

"Yes, Mavis, tell me about yourself."

Ow! Clarise say in her mind, glad bad that is not she the woman ask. Cause if was me I mustbe woulda have to start with when I did marry . . . at de queh-queh . . . wedding eve . . .

"Clarise! Is you de lady talking to. Is what happen to you?" Mavis say.

"No, I spoke to Mavis," the woman say, smiling.

"Yes, but I . . . but she . . . Ohhh God! Clar-*ise!*"

And is one hunch with Mavis elbow Clarise feel in her ribs before she say:

"Ohhh yes! Yes?"

The woman laugh-out-loud now.

"Why don't you two go and get it together? Decide which one's going to be Mavis and then come back . . . On second thought, no, don't bother. I'm sorry. I'm truly

66

sorry. Could I offer you a cup of coffee before you go? I'll have to ask you to make it yourself, but then . . . No, you'd best go. Thanks for coming. I really have to get back to work."

"I'm sor —"

BLADAM!

Is Mavis, the real one, start to tell the woman she sorry, but is slam the door slam in her face cause all the time the woman talking bout coffee she only inching inching to the door and them-two, Clarise and Mavis, moving backward and even the dog come and take his place so she could hold him by the collar and he could stare them down with that ignar look pon his face.

"Me? Hold he?" Clarise say to Mavis. "Not me! I never see a ugly beast like he. He —"

"Clarise! SHUT UP! Don't talk don't talk don't talk! DON'T TALK! I shame shame shame! And look! I might as well tell you this now, and forever after shut up with you. Listen! Listen good! In this country here? Clarise, y'don't see straydawg. Watch round! Watch round good. See if y'see any straydawg?"

"Is true, but y'know what, Mavis? Since thing get bad in Guyana —"

"WAIT LIL! Shut up! Wait lil! Listen to me! Shut up for a change and listen good. You know what that mean?"

"What what mean?"

"*Steewpps!* That you don't see any straydawg in New York, Clarise. God! You is a dunce or something? You know what that mean?"

"If I know what that mean? Chile? Since de crisis come in Guyana? One set of Chinese restaurant open pon Sheriff Street. Y'know? From de trainline to Duncan Street? Ow! Is a nice road now. Like a highway like

. . . that road alone have seventeen! Y'hear me? Seventeen Chinese restaurants. And y'know what, Mavis? Another thing happen. All them straydawg use to run out de backyard to bite your heel when you passing in them lil muddy sidestreet? Y'know how *any* street thatside had nuff nuff straydawg? Remember? All them son-a-dawg and rice-eater? Barking hard hard? Use to run out de yard? Remember, Mavis?"

"Yes yes, I remember, but Clarise, what —"

"Wait, Mavis! All them straydawg gone now . . . Gone, gone, disappear!"

"Clarise, you *joking,* I trying to tell you something."

"NO! I not joking! Not a straydawg. They mystic! Vanish without-a-trace, they —"

"Clarise, you don't see straydawg in New York cause people *own* de dawgs. That's why y'don't see straydawg in New York. And people don't make *joke* with they dawg here. That is all I have to say to you so you won't go on washing-your-mouth pon people dawg here. They don't have straydawg here with no owner, Clarise."

"It look to me like they have enough stray *people* with no owner here. Is what they going want with stray*dawg,* eh?"

"Hmmmmmmmmmmmm!" Is groan Mavis groaning. Mavis don't say another word, she just groan.

"I trying your nerves, nuh, chile?" Clarise say. "I am sorry. Sometimes I'm a trial to my ownself. But bear with me, please. I confuse. I ain't catch m'self yet. Is only brave I does play brave . . ."

Now look again!

Is Mavis stand-up by a ten-ton truck with her face set-up like rain coming cause this time Clarise have a

68

big-crowd round her. *Pure men* in the crowd and Clarise showing them Harold picture and smiling-up with them. Is everywhere Clarise taking out Harold picture and showing people and asking them if they see Harold.

"Is how people going to see Harold in big big New York, eh?" Mavis telling her. "And after all that talking on Tuesday morning? Watch what happening pon de road!"

The men in the crowd they smiling at Clarise and saying, "Hey, mama, what's your number? . . ."

Is now Mavis she look round and is so she grabbing Clarise hand and starting to run cross the road and all the time she saying fast fast, "Don't look back, Clarise. Don't look! Don't ask no questions. Just do what I tell you for once . . ."

And is so Clarise find herself scooting cross the road. And all the way she going, Clarise talking to herself and asking herself, Eh-eh! Is why you have to running for, Clarise chile? You thief something? You kill somebody or threaten to kill them? Eh-eh! So is why you have to running so?

But Clarise ain't saying nothing at all to Mavis. She is a mutchy-mutchy lady but she ain't no jungulung. She hustle cause she know Mavis is a very touchous lady. She been craking whole day bout this-and-that. If Clarise don't do what she say now? Be another ant-nest she stir up.

So Clarise run-no-ground till she reach cross the road and is now Mavis telling her she must go behind this clothesrack where she going find a man hiding from Andrew Grimes — who coming down the road!

So Clarise run quick quick behind the clothesrack where it too dark to see.

"Mister? You here? Move over lil bit, please . . ."

Clarise hear a groan and somebody saying:

"Oye oye oye! I done dead already now! Lawd! Lady, is what you doing here? This is a *private* property, y'know?"

Clarise turn to watch who talk to her and she see a face looking back at her hardly look older than her son Clarence who soon going in seventeen.

"Is where you from, son?"

"Trinidad, lady," the boy say and he groan again.

"I did say so! Last-year-Christmas Miz Jonson sister daughter come from Trinidad to spend time and is justso she singing her words when she talking, just like you . . ."

The boy moaning and groaning and Clarise ignoring him and talking:

"But is why you here hiding in this alley, son? If you was home in Trinidad is so you woulda been hiding in a alley like this?"

"I liming. Ah liming, lady," the boy say. Then he ask, "Mr. Grimes send you here to get me?"

"You not *liming* nowhere! You *hiding!*" Clarise say.

"Lady? You *mama-guying* me or what? You not serious? You come here to play picong?"

"Boy!" Clarise say sharp sharp like if she talking to Clarence. "Boy, you know I have a son just like you? Don't talk to me full-mouth so. Not cause I look so. I'm a *big-woman,* hear? I could be your *mother. Is what you hiding in this alley for?*"

"Lady, this is not no alley. This here is Seventh Avenue."

"This is not no avenue! This is a dirty alley and you is nothing but a alleyrat if you don't come out from hiding underneath these clothes under this clothesrack. Is what you frighten so? Tell me, is who you frighten?"

The poor boy left so! with his mouth open. He can't talk. He too surprise. His mouth opening and shutting like fish-outa-water and is so his eye pulping out his head.

"Is cause you don't have greencard? Is that? But that is not no sin. Don't let nobody fool you tell you that is a sin cause you don't have a lil piece of plastic. Tell me why you shouldn't free to walk de world if you have de money to pay your way, eh? Tell me why all people shouldn't free to walk everywhere?"

The boy make to get up.

"No, boy!" Clarise say. "Listen me! Hear me now! You getting up and face that man and —"

"Ohhh my Lawd! I done dead already! Lady, if you is a Babylon-bannas please go fight somewhere else cause I ain't digging that now, okay?" the boy say, cause he peep through the London Fogs and he see . . .

"Why you running from that man?" Clarise ask.

"Cause he going to kill me!" the boy say.

"Why you think he going kill you?"

"Sou-sou . . . I push him too far," the boy say. "But lady? Lady, who is you? Is why you asking me so much questions for? Lady, I in *plenty* trouble. Please go away. What you doing here? Why you here?"

"Cause my friend tell me . . . But boy! I thought de man only suppose to give you to immigration. Is how you think he going kill you? And what is this bout sou-sou?" Clarise ask the boy.

"Excuse me lil bit, lady. I a lil busy . . . I gone, hear?" The boy try to get up.

"No! You not gone yet! Wait!"

Clarise pull him down.

"Boy? One of these days you not going have no place to run to. Is what you going do then, eh?"

"Then is saldering time lady, saldering time . . ."

"Don't run, boy . . . Wait! Why you running? All they could do if they catch you is put you pon a plane and send you home. What wrong with that?"

"How you mean 'what wrong with that,' lady? Is there I just come from. I don't know what you mean by 'put me on a plane' . . . And I don't know where *you* come from, lady."

"Boy, where you live in Trinidad?"

"SeaLots, lady. People say Trinidad rich cause it have oil. And Eric Williams did say oil don't spoil. But it still have people catching arse in Trinidad. And is not *every*body *like it so* and don't want to move out."

"But you not telling me nothing! I come from *Guyana!* You know bout there?"

"Lady, all I know is what I hear, that Guyana *nearly* like Jamaica. But I not digging that now. Is here I have to get out of now before . . ."

The Trinidadian boy peep through the London Fogs again and Clarise peep too.

Is Mavis coming down from the other side of the street cussing-to-ground with a man, but he not paying her no attention. His head still swiveling like turkey neck.

"Lemme tell you a thing or so, Mr. Andrew Grimes . . ."

So *that* is de Andrew Grimes? Clarise say to herself. Well look how people could dress-up nice and be long-hearted so, eh?

Mavis cussing-out:

"Well, if you not following me and my friend, then is that poor man over there . . ."

"Where? Over there? Over there where? Where is he? Show him to me! Where is the little reprobate?"

"Don't use me with words! Don't give me all that big-English in your mouth. You meaning that *poor il-legal alien* over there? Yes, is that what we does call them poor birds like de ones hiding behind de clothes. They name *illegal aliens* and you name *chickenhawk*."

"Clothes? Where? Sooo! That's where he's hiding . . . *Now* we shall see!"

Andrew Grimes is a man does walk with a limp and is so he half-walking-half-running and limping cross the road, not even taking Mavis on.

You could tell Andrew Grimes mind on the clothes-rack cause his eyes focus on it. But all he seeing is a set of coats. He can't see what going on behind there. He don't know that through the London Fogs the boy eyes make four with his eyes. Andrew Grimes don't know that that boy don't know that he Andrew Grimes can't even see him.

And the boy start to panic:

"Look, lady! I not joking now! Lehgo-me, hear? Lehgome! Lemme go! Let me go!"

The boy tug away his hand from Clarise who get take unawares cause she only watching Andrew Grimes and shaking her head in her mind and saying:

Eh-eh! See-me-not-live-with-me, yeah! Is true true story that Mammie does talk. Look how that man dress-up and look how his face look like a kind and good person. And is what he doing to live?

Eh-eh!

Clarise looking through the Fogs seeing Mavis coming down on the man heels cussing through:

"*Reprobate*? You know what you sound like? Mister chickenhawk? Mister headhunter? Mister . . . Andrew Grimes? You sound like a real Brigah-Johnny, that is what you sound like. But lemme tell you something. Listen good! Every Mouthouse like you should know this. *'That thing what sweeten goat-mouth does hurt he belly,'* hear?"

Eh-eh! Clarise left stunned watching Mavis wagging-up her finger in the man face and shaking-up herself and . . . Eh-eh! If was Clarise getting-on so Mavis woulda done tell her how she too braddar and that this is New York not Guyana and you can't get-on so here.

Clarise peeping through the London Fogs at Mavis enjoying her abuse when she feel the tug on her hand. Is the boy stand up sudden and cant over the clothesrack and the whole thing come down pon her and the boy fall down pon top of it and her.

Clarise don't even know why she fighting-up so hard to keep the boy there till the man reach them but she start to tumble with the boy, trying to get his hand back. But now that boy ain't making joke. He getting desperate. He fighting and he begging at the same time.

"Ow, lady, you making skylark or what? Lemme go now, please? Lemme go? It have a thing name *mercy*. Have mercy pon me, lady. If Mr. Grimes catch me he will *kill* me this time. Lady, lady . . . lady . . . lady you know I could . . . I might . . . I . . ."

Is one big-cuff the boy fold close to Clarise nose like if he threatening her. He raise his free hand and he coming down with the cuff. Clarise watch him hard and say:

"You wouldn't dare do that to me!" sharp sharp sharp.

"You see?" he say. "You see you see you see, lady? You see how like you come here to play mother pon me? Lady, *you are not* my mother. I left my mother in Trinidad by SeaLots there. Is where you come from? I never leave Trinidad till I come to New York. I never had Guyanese mother. I never set foot in Guyana so I never see you before in my whole life. You not even *Trinidadian* self. Why you want to take over my life so? Boy-oh-boy! This is a . . . a . . . Look! Lehgo me, lehgo

74

me! *Lemme go!*" the boy say, and with that he make one big-tug and get his hand free. "Christ!" he say, "and the damn woman have the grip of a giant! Bull-shit! FUCKIT! You not my mother, lady!"

And the boy dash down the London Fog he pull off his head pon Clarise head before he take off down the road like rabbit-outa-hole.

"Boy! Come back! Don't run away! Boy? Wait! Is not so to face life. This life could better than home? That hell is your *own* hell, boy. Wait! Take it from me. I only here less than a week and I know, I see already this life couldn't better . . ."

Is a good thing Seventh Avenue always got traffic-jam or that poor boy woulda lick-up heself under some taxi or ten-ton truck or something. Cause he *late!* He late to get away from Clarise still roll up in the London Fogs pon the ground bawling after him. He late to get away from Andrew Grimes who coming-on limping fast, passing Clarise.

"Come back, boy. I know I'm not your mother but I'm talking to you like my own son . . ."

Clarise look up and see Andrew Grimes. "And as for *you,* sir, you is another-one. Mr. Grimes, is you I'm talking to . . ."

"Do I know you?" Andrew Grimes stop. He look back at Clarise, he hesitate, and then he say while he limping away:

"Sorry, I can't help you now. If you're still here when I come back I'll help you, but right now I have some business with —"

"G'wan, you ole lampy-pampy-junketteh! Y'will *never* catch up with him."

Is Mavis!

"Ow, Mavis. *Any*body could have break-foot. Y'have

75

to cuss him for that, too?" Clarise say from the ground, where she just relax now in the mess-up coats.

"Look, Clarise, you don't get me wild. That man is a dirty dawg! *You* don't know he. If I had de will o' he? I would . . . I would . . . And too-besides, is all your fault."

"Me? *My* fault, Mavis? I did exactly what you say to me. I ain't ask no questions, I do what you say. I come to this clothesrack and I find a boy behind it. Unless you mean de lil discourse I meet up with here? But you weren't here, you don't know what we talk bout . . ."

"Clarise, is when you going get serious, eh? Look! De day done already, is nearly four o'clock. Is de *whole* week done too and you ain't even find a job yet. Like *all* you concentrating pon is finding Harold Cumberbatch. You have to find *work,* Clarise, if you want to do *any-thing* in this country you have to have money. That lil twenty-five dollars de government give you to walk with done de first day you come. Y'self *see* that. All de Guyana money you bring is no use here. You coulda spend your money and enjoy y'self with it in Guyana, cause you can't buy nothing with it here, they not changing it at de bank. I tell you that before, but like you still have hopes."

"But we didn't try *all* de banks, Mavis, you mean they don't have *one?* Is a whole *thousand* dollars I save . . ."

"Look, Clarise, get up from de ground, come, lehwe go along, hear? You talking *pure* foolishness. Guyana money is *Monopoly* money. I done tell you that already. I ain't able waste my breath no more. That is for children to play Monopoly games with. Come along."

"Lady, that sofa of coats you're stretched out on

happens to be Macy's property. What's going on here, anyway? Where's the boy?" Neither Mavis nor Clarise see the man when he walk up.

Mavis say, "A man name Grimes chase him away."

"Grimes? Jesus! *Grimes again?* You mean Andrew Grimes? Guy's got a limp and wears a hat?"

"That *same* one, that same so-and-so!" Mavis say.

"Sheeeeit! Time's come I gotta make sure people who work for me don't owe Grimes no money before I hire 'em. That's the way I lose 'em all."

He stretch out his hand to help Clarise get up, he look at the coats on the ground and groan. He is a big-fatman who have on singlet-shirt in that cold cold weather. He run his hand through his thin gray-hair and he groan again.

"I can't take much more of this. Look! Just look at this merchandise, just look at it. *They* think it's a god-damn game or something, but I get into trouble every time with —"

"Game? What game?" Mavis ask the man. "How anybody could call selling people to immigration a game?"

"Who's selling who to immigration?" the man saying while he picking up his clothesrack.

"Andrew Grimes! He! Is that he does do. Sell poor illegal people to immigration . . . Like that boy if he catch him. He's a *chickenhawk,* that Andrew Grimes!"

"Chicken hawk? Selling people to who? Grimes? Hell no! If he would do *head-hunting* for a living he would be better off. He knows 'em all. But Grimes, he has a soft heart for West Indians and Africans in New York. I know the man, I met him when he was making his money bringing shoes from Brazil and carvings from Haiti. He ain't no head-hunter . . . what you call it?

77

Chicken hawk? He keeps their money for them, something like that. Anyhow, he ends up advancing them more than they ever pay back. He's a bad banker, in other words. Beats me how he's been able to keep it up all these years. That's how he got his limp, got knocked over by a car trying to catch a woman who owed him some money and was splitting the scene . . .

"But he keeps it up. That dude? The one's got me in this mess here? Let's say Grimes catches up with him. Know what'll happen? The guy'll sell him some jive story about having to send money to Jamaica or whatever. And my man Grimes, he'll take the five dollars the guy'll give him with the story, when he should be demanding twenty-five or fifty, and the game'll go on next payday. Wanna bet?

"He does this all over New York. It's a game — been playing it for *years* and he loves it. The damn fool! He gets taken again and again. Different strokes for different folks, I guess, and then again, as he likes to point out, them folks is *his people*. Beats me how . . . I just wish the muthafucka would keep them away from me, is all. They ain't *my* people and they ain't working for me no more. Just keep 'em away from . . ."

The man finish picking up his mess-up coats and hanging them on his clothesrack and is gone he gone rolling off with it without so much as a goodbye to Clarise and Mavis. Is like if he was talking to heself from the first, just like he talking to heself when he roll away . . .

"Ohhh! Is that what de boy was talking bout when he say de man going kill him for sou-sou? Is *boxhand* he throwing with Mr. Grimes? Ohhh . . ." And is so Clarise shaking her head and more sorry now she let that boy get away.

"Y'know what, Mavis? All of us coulda get to-gether, you and me and Mr. Grimes, and talk to that boy and teach him to face up to his responsibility. He can't go along so in life, he has to learn —"

"Look, Clarise, come along, lehwe go, hear? I going home. I tired. You always with some stupidness."

Clarise open her mouth to tell Mavis something, to ask her *what* stupidness, but she change her mind cause she see Mavis in a bad mood.

Is only cause she shame, Clarise say to herself. She shame cause she make a big-mistake and Clarise know how the surprise affect her friend. Cause all the time the fatman was talking? Mavis left so listening with her mouth open.

Is shame she shame . . .

On the train going home Clarise silent like Mavis and the rest of the people. A man open the door and come in from another passengercar with a ole tincup in his hand singing some ole song bout you hold up your head in the storm and don't let the dark scare you. His clothes tear up and dirty, he smelling bad! He begging . . . When anybody put anything in the tincup? He stop in front of them and finish his song. Clarise can hear the coins going ping-pong ping-pong when somebody put something inside.

But she can tell that some people don't want to give nothing. They frighten of him, they don't want him to come and stand-up in front of them and sing noth-ing.

Clarise start to open her purse.

Mavis turn, watch her, and let out a long breeze but she don't say nothing.

Clarise drop her twenty-five cents in the man tincup, *ping!* and he start to sing bout the same ole story and the sky does turn to gold . . .

Is how long since you hear that song? Clarise ask herself. That is a ole ole song . . .

That man was a good singer in his days, a good good singer . . . He is still a good singer. I wonder what happen to him? Clarise say in her mind.

"Thanks, sir. I enjoy de song," Clarise say, and the man walk on with the coins in his tincup going jingle-jangle-jangle and people playing like they not seeing him, just like if they frighten to watch him.

Eh-eh! But is why they frighten to watch de poor man? His clothes rag-up, yes, he smell lil frowsy f'truth, yes. But what? He only earning a daily bread. He ain't really begging nobody. He singing and he getting pay for his song. Is why they all so fraid de poor man? He mustbe *de dark* or something, that's why everybody so frighten of him.

"Mavis, I didn't get to de end of de story bout de pittites when you call me that day on de subway and de young man had to get off, remember? It just come back to me now. Y'know —"

"Clarise, not now . . . Please . . ."

So Clarise don't worry to tell Mavis, but she sit down staring in space like everybody else on the train and she remembering that the time does come when even the pittites begging starboy to ease up pon the man he beating up. Like, "Done, now. Stop! You want to kill he or what? Ow! Stop now, man, stop!" And if something happen and starboy get kill? Everybody going home disappoint cause nobody don't like no picture that starboy die in. They say starboy don't die. They leaving the cinema and they stewpsing stewpsing, sucking-up they teeth. They depress. *Steewpps!* Is how starboy could die, eh? Who ever hear bout starboy he dead?

Is just like if they don't know, they don't understand, that if starboy don't want to get heself kill, he
have to be cruel with the blows. He *can't* stop. He have
to kill. He is the one that have to do the killing if he
want to be starboy cause is that what make him starboy
in the first place . . .

Seven

Okay, Clarise, you know de place a lil bit now so you on your own. You not going have Mavis Drakes to driving crazy in de New York streets no more. But take a lil advice: when you looking for a job and you go to de agencies? Please don't talk so much. You sounding just like a just-come and as soon as de people spot that they going ask you for greencard.

"Anyway, you still have mine, but only use it if you *have* to use it. Try everything else first, and f'Godsake! *Remember* what is your name and try to talk a lil *English* sometimes. People here don't understand this Guyanese you talking all de time so."

But Clarise tell Mavis that she prefer to sound like a just-come instead of a been-away cause them been-aways always sounding like they swallow they tongue or something. Is one heavy accent they does pick up, them B.A.

82

"One of them, a B.A., he come back after only *three months* in America and he get deport. Before day-morning he stand-up pon his mother frontsteps bramming down de door, baddabambam, calling out, 'Maum? Maum, owpen ze daur, will ya? Maum, et's meh, your sohn. Et's Herebert! Owpen up!'

"Eh-eh! De po' ole lady wake up with de sleep in her eye hearing this thing. She say to herself, 'Take care is not thiefman tricks!' cause she ain't understanding a word de boy saying. He sounding like her son Herbert, but Herbert gone to America, he couldn't here, she say to herself.

"But she throw a piece ole cloth over her head for de dew, she push open de window, poke out her head, and call out, 'A-who that?' 'Et's meh, Maum, Herebert!' he say. 'Eh-eh! Is Erbert in truth!'

"De ole lady put on de landing light over de front step. She wake up her husband: 'Is Erbert come, but de boy sounding strange, he sounding funny.'

"She open de door. 'Ow, m'son? m'son?' De ole lady pull her boy head down on her bosom. 'Son, is why you come back so quick? And is what they do to you in America make you can't talk plain no more?' "

When Clarise finish telling Mavis the story, she throw back her head and laugh hearty. But Mavis don't say a word. She just put on her shoes, take her coat out the cupboard by the door, and when she finish buttoning it up she say:

"Okay, Clarise. Is all right, chile. I *glad* you can laugh. But remember! In *this* country — or *anywhere*, for that matter, even in *your* beloved Guyana — *when money done, fun done.* And they don't give job to no just-come here before they give to a been-away. Especially if de B.A. have greencard and de just-come ain't got none. Goodbye, Clarise, good luck. I late this morning and I gone . . ."

Well, Clarise, you don't want to hear it plainer than that, girl. What Mavis just tell you is that she ain't got no more money to give you or lend you, whichever one she call it. You on your own in this hard-as-ass place. And you late, too. You shoulda been out de house with Mavis but like you don't want to go . . . But you *have* to go, Clarise, you *have* to go. What else y'going do, eh?

Is *you* make up your bed, love. Is not you have to lie down pon it? Nobody done send and call you here to New York. Hurry, chile, is nearly seven-thirty, and remember to dress warm. Cause de man say pon de radio that it going be forty-five degrees today, and that cold. Don't worry with them saying that de weather warming up. It *cold-as-ass* today! Dress warm, chile. Put on one them funny longdrawers Mavis lend you to save the expense of buying for y'self. Well *look* what you come to, eh? You have to borrow people drawers. Mavis is your friend, but still . . .

Steewpps!

But console y'self, chile, is not drawers, f'truth. You have on your own panty underneath this one. This one here name longjohn and yours name panty. Mavis calling it jukebox cause it big and comfortable. She say, *"Ow, Clarise, panty cheap here, buy two good-looking drawers, nuh? That thing look like it come from home."*

But f'what? Buy drawers for what? These here ole but they clean and they comfortable and they ain't got no hole. And I don't have no man to be taking them off for. So nobody but me know they not fancy. And Mavis. But she is my friend, she could forgive me. I ain't buying *nothing* here I don't have to buy. I will buy lil hard-to-get items for my children at home . . . And even down to that, even *that* I can't see my way yet to . . .

84

Good! Now put on de — thermal does they call it? — underwear top. And put on de longsleeves-sweater and put on de cardigan and . . .

Ow, girl! Watch how you look like a big-fat ole woman, eh? Now you have to put on *coat* pon top of this? But *do* it, chile, do it. Is for your *own* comfort. Don't worry with them saying de weather warming up. To you it cold cold cold *still*. Is that wind you can't stand. Like it does boring through to your bone-marrow.

Now! Where de gloves? But first find de lil woolhat that does come down over your ears and de long-wool-scarf for your neck, *then* you put on de gloves. And find your umbrella, cause they say it might rain, and . . . Oh! De boots? Or shoes?

Lemme see.

Ow Lawd! It raining already. And de snow that fall yesterday? Mix up with this rain now turning into . . .

Put on your boots, Clarise. Take off de shoes and put on de boots . . . *Boots, boots, de government boots* . . . Cause is left-right-left-right you going have to going through all that weather again . . .

All right, chile. New York ready.

Ow God! Is who is who is who you? Is where you there? Is why you deserting me so? All I ask is that you help me make it through today. I ready, Lawd! I will take it one day at a time. Matthew Allen, boy, I miss your morning-song pon de radio every morning quarter-to-seven:

"I'm only human, I'm just a woman. Help me to see what I can be and all that I am. Show me the stair-way I have to climb. And for my sake, teach me to take, one day at a time . . . One day at a time, sweet Jesus, that's all I'm asking of you. Just show me the way to do every day what I have to do. Yesterday's gone, sweet Jesus, tomorrow may never be mine . . ."

Lawd? Is where in this Christ-world Harold Cumberbatch find heself? I getting tired looking for he already and I ain't even start good yet. Is only one week I
here and like is a whole lifetime I live here already. This
place so big and confuse it make me feel small small
small. But I will go on, I have to . . . One-day-at-a-time
I will go on. I can't buy no more pictures. They too dear.
But enough people have now and they beginning to call
me and tell me . . . Lawd! if you want me to find him?
I know I will . . . and a job!

Is Clarise walking out Mavis house that Monday
morning singing her song and talking to herself and
hoping and praying.

Mavis right.

Clarise coulda find a proper job sooner if she didn't
have to looking for Harold all over the place. And what?
Is all kinds of wild-goose-chase people sending her pon.
The trouble is, she can't refuse to go, cause suppose the
same time she refuse is the *one* time is Harold she going
find in truth? New York too big for her to be going all
over Queens and Brooklyn and Bronx when the morning come to check out information that people who *sure*
they see Harold give her, and still keep appointments
to find work.

Is not only that it big . . . is the traffic when she
decide to take the busway. I never see so much confusion in my *whole life,* Clarise does say to herself when
day-after-day she sitting down in the bus inching along
to some address so far away she can't walk and go.

And if she take the subway?

Is changing trains at Forty-second Street crossing
over platform at Fulton Street taking the local and not
the express at Franklin staying at the back of the train
so she could climb up to the street in the right place
when the train stop. Too much! Too much too much.

One time she get a wink that it have a cleaning-job on Fulton Street. And when she get off the train she start walking. She walking walking walking, but like the address disappear off the street. She decide to ask somebody to help her. Then is when she finding out that Fulton Street is like Supernaam to Charity in Guyana or New Amsterdam to Corriverton. You can't go looking for address on Essequibo Coast or Berbice Road if you don't know the direct area you looking for in Guyana. But still you could reach-up somebody who know somebody, who related to the body you looking for. And is so you going get help. But here? Nobody don't care and they don't know to say *I don't know,* either. Ask somebody in New York a direction and they will give you it even if they don't know a damn thing they talking bout.

Is so Clarise getting loss, but she learning the place and meeting people, and now she don't have Mavis quarreling-up with her? She can stop and talk to whoever she want and give hot-mouth to whoever vex her.

Like the man in this lil shop on Delancey Street . . .

Clarise go in the shop to buy some Vaseline to send home to comb her children hair, and a tube of toothpaste. She say she might as well buy it now cause she know the way things going she not going have money to steady sending home things and she glad she could get a eighteen-dollar bottle of petroleum jelly for a dollar-and-something here. As for the toothpaste? When she home and she don't have money to buy any she could just go out in the backyard and pick a piece of black-sage. That does clean her and the children teeth cleaner and whiter than any toothpaste.

But since it so cheap here she decide to buy it.

Clarise count-up the money and it come to three-

dollars-and-something when she finish buying everything. She buy a cake of soap, too. But when the man
ring the bell the register say that she owe him four dollars and fifteen cents.

Eh-eh!

"Is how is that, mister?" Clarise ask.

"How is what?" the man say.

"How is so much when this is one dollar and fifty-
four and this is . . ."

"You ever heard of a thing called tax, lady?"

"Tax? What tax?"

"New York City sales tax."

"I don't understand . . . You mean pon top of de
price you have to pay more?"

How come she didn't notice this before? Clarise girl?
You must learn to count your money more better. Like
all this time you been getting rob and you didn't even
know.

"Not me, you. I didn't buy anything," the man say.
"You have to pay eight-and-a-quarter percent tax."

"But why?"

Now the man can't control heself no more.

"So Uncle Sam can afford to keep *all you illegal
aliens* in America!"

"Who Uncle Sam? All what illegal aliens?"

"Aliens . . . illegal . . . like you. Ain't you illegal?"

Eh-eh!

But look story! Look how this man making he eyes
to pass me? Is how he know I'm a . . . But he can't be
one them chickenhawk Mavis tell me bout? Evenso, he
making me sound like I just drop out de sky from *Mars*
or something, like I ain't got owner . . .

And really-and-truly I don't have no relatives here,
Clarise say to herself. If I did have any Uncle Sam here
I won't so po'-like-church-rat now, with this one here

robbing me too. My uncle woulda give me some money . . .

"Mister! I tell you something. You think is you only one got country? You think I just drop from de sky? You think I here cause I love this place? I here nearly two months now, and I know already this ain't no easy place to be if you want to make a life. Not cause Guyana in a mess you could insult me so. It ain't going stay so forever.

"And too-besides —"

Eh-eh!

Clarise taking out the fold-up money from her purse while the man watching and waiting and she saying to herself, If he want it, he has to *wait* for it. But too-besides? No! He can't cussing me out so and still expects to get my money. He can't cussing me so and expects me to buy from he.

Justso?

No!

Clarise making up her mind not to take the things when the man say:

"Guyana? Didn't that place used to be British Guyana?"

"Yes . . . so what? We *independent* now, we ain't no *British* now. We po' but we ind —"

"Hell, if it weren't for the British you people would still be swinging from trees."

Eh-eh!

But look story!

Clarise watch round to see who hearing, if anybody in the shop *hearing* her trial this good day. But all the people playing like they not hearing. A woman just outside the door jump when she see Clarise looking round for help and she walk away fast.

Eh-eh!

Well, is everybody thinking like this man then? Or else somebody woulda tell he that he talking stupidness when he say if was not for the British people in Guyana we woulda still *swinging in trees*? Is *that* he really say though?

Eh-eh!

Is what he talking at all? He ain't even making sense. He couldn't serious. Watch he in he face good, see if he serious, Clarise . . .

He serious, yes!

Eh-eh!

"I don't want these things no more!" Clarise say, and she turn the bag the man put the things in upside-down. She just lift up the bag and the toothpaste and the petroleum jelly go *bopplap* pon de shop-counter and the petroleum jelly roll away. He had to grab it fast before it fall pon de shop-floor.

"I don't-need-it-no-more. And evenself I need it, I don't *want* it nomore. I will do without it. You can't cussing me out so and expects me to spend my money in your store. I will do without it . . .

"And I-tell-you-more-something you ole sakka-bakka-rass-hole . . ."

Eh-eh! But is what is this at all?

Clarise never did cuss so for a long time, not even in Guyana where cuss does break out justso for less than this . . . *far* less than this.

"I did know a man *just like you* . . . Estate-man-ager. He come to my country with a *bug-house* pon he head and a grip with not-one-shit-in-it. All he had was de few clothes pon he back. Same thing with his wife . . . I had a auntie use to work for them. She use to tell we how de mistress use to tell her — when she not bragahing pon her — how they *never* had it so good in

England where they come from. Never had it so good till they come to Guyana . . . Was British Guyana then . . .

"But *not* he! He was one *prepostik big-shot*. Y'would think he born-with-silver-spoon-in-he-mouth. Nothing was never good enough for him there . . ."

Eh-eh!

Clarise talking fast and breathing hard.

"But we live to see de day Independence come and not long after that? That same man had to pack his grip — full this time — and leave my country. He cry-he-heart-out! I see with these two eyes . . . I just a young girl going school, passing home from school that day and my auntie call me and I see he crying tears, hear? Is only now I get big I putting-two-and-two-to-gether . . .

"If de place and de people was so *stinking,* as he use to say, is why? Why he couldn't go-back-where-he-come-from without de waterworks, eh? Is why he did want to stay?

"What ain't pass you ain't miss you, hear, mister? Y'hearing what I saying? What miss you ain't pass you, too! Cause *you* ain't sounding like no *American* to me."

The man stand-up watching Clarise with his mouth open like he fascinate.

"I don't understand a *word* you're saying," he tell her, turning to the last customer left in the store, cause everybody else walk out while the cuss-out going on.

"Well is not *my* fault you stupidy. Don't blame *me* cause you stupidy. I understand all *you* say to *me.*"

And Clarise flounce out the store.

Eight

I**s true!**

In America they don't give no just-come no job in front a been-away. Especially when the B.A. got green-card and the J.C. ain't got none. Even if they offer you a job they saying: "Bring your greencard along with you." And that is where they got you.

It take Clarise months to find a proper job. Was a lil baby-sitting thing here or a lil hold-on cleaning-up in a giftshop there.

One time she get a lil job in Long Island with a woman who was *clean out her head*. A big ole house this woman living in, with a grandfather-clock chirping all hours and playing church music and Clarise is her home attendant.

And all hours of the night when that clock strike, this woman getting dress-up — black dress, black veil, black boots — and she calling Clarise: "Come, it's time to go to church."

Sometimes poor Clarise would wake out her deep deep sleep, middle-of-the-night, and that woman standing over her, black dress, black veil, black boots, and the grandfather-clock striking and playing church music . . .

"Come, Clarise, it's time to go to church . . ."

That job last for three days. Yet still, the madwoman not as bad as them some of who think they sane. Like the one who want poor Clarise to put on white-uniform-and-shoe to clean her house. When Clarise ask her for the money to buy the white-uniform-and-shoe? She get chase out the woman house.

And is so she loss *that* one.

And like she not getting through with anything good when she show Mavis greencard. She say to herself is not that they don't believe her, mustbe something bout her that making them lose interest even before they see the greencard.

Or mustbe not true that they don't look careful and all o' we look alike?

Is over six weeks gone now and she ain't get a job yet. She bring twenty-five U.S. dollars to America with her. That is all the government let her have . . . her allowance for a whole year to travel with. But Clarise didn't know that the lil savings she put together and her mother help her with was going be no use to her here.

Steewpps! Y'have money in your purse and y'can't spend it! So what is de use of de money? And if you try to bring out lil gold, they stopping you at de airport.

Clarise hear that gold could spend *anywhere* in the world, even here. And *look* how much gold Guyana got.

Plenty plenty plenty gold. Is her gold earring and the chain and the bangles Clarise pawn that still keeping her with the lil help Mavis give her and the lil babysitting work and so now and then.

But you can't bring out the gold justso. Y'does have to hide some, and if they catch you? . . . You know how much people getting jail when they search them at the airport and finding the gold hide away in all parts of de person?

Steewpps! But that is to show how much you know, Clarise. You don't know nothing if you don't know Guyana money not good nowhere else but in Guyana. Not *one* bank over here would take it. You coulda save y'self de trouble. Now y'have one thousand *useless* dollars and just this few-cents left from all the pawnings and borrowings and struggling-through-the-weather to work for three-fifty a hour.

"Hey, foxy mama, you wanna join my stable?"

Clarise look round and she see a man with a ballhead like Isaac Hayes stand-up bowing and dancing-up pon his two feet and smiling-up at her.

Eh-eh!

Well is what is he case? Like he got Saint-Vitus-Dance or something.

"Mister, if you looking for a horse name Clarise? This ain't de one, hear?"

"Ohhh, Clarise, mama, but you look like one *fine* mare to me."

Come to think bout it, I could be a kiss-my-ass *mule,* f'truth, the way I fetching load since I know m'self good. And don't *talk* bout these days . . .

But time running out. You better hustle chile — oh, but Mavis say that you mustn't say *hustle* cause it mean only one thing. Well, I ain't ready for that yet. Push going really have to come to shove first, and that

94

ain't happen yet. So I going say what I say to myself. I *hustling* in my own way without belonging to anybody *stable*.

But is not so it suppose to be in America? What happen to me? Is goat bite me? Is thief I thief Jesus boots or something? All my luck run out since I come to America. But de ole people say you suppose to change your luck when you cross water. And pon top of that I was *always* like wild-eddoe: cut me down today, I spring up tomorrow. Is what gone wrong, eh?

Eh-eh!

This country like a blasted *cross!*

Is that.

It nice, yes, but it hard baaad! It so blasted hard y'can't even *see* it nice sometimes. Is all sort of full-eye things to make you sorry for y'self in your hand-to-mouth existence. Watch at all-them things in de glass-case! Is when I ever going able buy anything so?

Steewpps!

Clarise talking to herself cool cool cause she know nobody digging cause is not she alone carrying on big-big-conversation with herself pon the road in New York. And people just passing them and nobody ain't taking them on.

Is only now people in Guyana getting accustom to madpeople, cause you seeing them more and more and more. They taking off they clothes and exposing they-self. They skinning-and-grinning. They walking walking walking. They talking in the streets. They gone-off with the pressure.

But I didn't know it have so much pressure *here,* cause it look like it have more madpeople here than sane ones, Clarise say to herself. Like is not only work you don't have, or husband gone-away-left-you, or no food to eat, is all does send you crazy here . . .

Clarise walking down Fifth Avenue talking to herself and watching all the store-dolly dress-up in nice
clothes staring at she.

Watch them! Just watch how they dress-to-death.
Ow, Clarise chile, is when is when is when you going
ever get to wear a velvetskirt and shinyblouse like them,
eh?

Eh-eh!

Look at this one! She lay down, stretch out, relax.
Y'see, chile? Relax. When you relax your *physical*, your
mind and everything in your life does run right.

Ow, Clarise chile, here, turn down this corner see
what you could find down here.

But is where you going? You know where you
going? Clarise, you looking for a *job*, not wandering in
your mind, hear?

Look! Stop here. Here nice. It wide-and-open-and-
nice. You can see the *skies* here . . .

Is where? . . . God in de heavens, in de mountains, lift up your head . . .

Guyana!

Is what that sign doing on lantern-post in New York?
Here is where? Avenue of de Americas? West Forty-six
Street? What Guyana doing here? Ohhh, but is not
Guyana alone . . .

And so Clarise walking calling out the names of
the countries on the lantern-posts till she catch herself
loss, talking to herself:

It is one thing I did know in school is my geography . . . But Clarise, you better forget geography
and do lil *arithmetic* lil. Is how much money in your
purse?

"Would you like to attend a *free* show at CBS this
morning?"

Clarise turn round at the words and she see they

coming from under a lil round-rim-stingy-brim-blue-cloth hat on a head with a Chinese face and eyes. The woman say:

"They're testing a show for audience reaction. Wanna go?"

"Me? Yes, thanks . . . What is a CBS, though?"

And a man passing-by call out:

"That's congenital brain syndrome, lady."

But the lady under the hat say:

"Forget that weirdo. It's a television network in . . . Where you from?"

"Guyana," Clarise say.

"Oh. Don't bother, then."

"Why?"

"They need people who have a New York address."

"I have one. I work for de person in charge of de *New York Times* papers."

"Oh, great! Here, take this, quick. You have to go now. The screening begins in five minutes. Fifty-second Street, go through the swinging doors. This is your pass . . ."

Clarise take the pass and start to hustle. The woman call out after her:

"Hey, you really going, huh? That means I get credit . . ."

Clarise leave her there gleaming like full-moon and she break-she-foot down the road to get to that place in time.

Is a line of people on a corner. Is plenty plenty people in uniform, like guards. Is a man walking up to Clarise saying:

"Come to the screening?"

"Yes, sir."

"Wait in the line over there . . ."

. . .

A hour later Clarise out in the streets again walking and stewpsing:

Clarise, you mustbe rich-and-idle, that's why you could waste all that time with all them people who go in there to press button and write-up form and watch foolishness pon de TV screen.

But is what she get?

Is a show name "The George Burns Comedy Hour."

And is shooting-up and killing-up. And they expect you to laugh at that?

Is some men tell they wives that they going fishing, but instead they take a airplane and gone to another country to hunt down some *dangerous criminal.*

Is violence and lies!

She write pon de paper: "People die not funny. It sad." And she go away left de place.

Eh-eh!

Clarise stewpsing up her teeth.

But justso there is one *nice* thing bout this place. It don't have too much *fast*people always watching you and minding your business for you.

But suppose you was to get sickness in this country? And you don't have nobody or no money?

This here is one *frightening* place, hear? Them don't care bout nobody else but theyself . . . What I want to know is why all o' we does *run come* here and is why them what come like me don't write home de truth. From how they does tell it is *everybody* doing well . . .

Is shame, is that. Is shame they does shame to talk de truth. Cause you not suppose to come to America to fail. Harold? Where you? Is how you doing?

Clarise pull out her list of places to go to from her coatpocket, walking and talking still:

I wonder if I was to confess that I don't have no

greencard what would happen? Cause this greencard thing with Mavis face pon it getting pon my nerves. Mavis is a *redwoman*. If I can see that in de picture is why them people not going see it?

. . . Confess and tell de person that interviewing me my whole story and ask her understanding . . . It must have somebody somewhere here with a heart who will listen to my distress . . .

I will try, Clarise say, and she look pon her paper for the next address she have to go to on the list that Mavis help her to take out the *New York Times*. All scratch off except two.

She going go to the last one first.

Is on the third floor, Forty-first Street near the corner.

Is a hardface girl sitting at a desk in front with powder and lipstick and rouge paste-up her face and her eyelash like tarantula-spider-leg. She squinting-up her face say she smiling at Clarise and asking if she could help her.

Is a roomful of people waiting, but Clarise ain't watching cause she don't want to see nobody look like she know them. Cause *she* can't stay so. She going *have* to give them a call-off. She can't make that playing-like-if-y'ain't-seeing thing. Not she Clarise. No!

"Can I help you?"

Is the hardface woman ask her again and is now. Is now is now is now so. Is now you have to tell her, Clarise . . . Go on, tell her and see if in this country it don't have nobody with a heart that soft and kind enough to help you out your distress . . .

But if this one heart soft, her face not showing it . . .

Is tell Clarise telling herself that mustbe not a good idea to confess now, not to this one. The face she imagine confessing to was one like the lil artistwoman in Queens. Or Mavis have a friend name Bella, that they meet-up pon de road last week and Mavis introduce her to. Bella does laugh hearty-and-deep and she look like you could tell her *anything* you have pon your mind. And she come from here, too. She is American. Only thing is, Clarise ain't had to ask nobody who look like Bella or herself Clarise self for a job since she come to this country. Is pure people like this hardface woman what squinting to laugh, and that artistwoman. Pure whitepeople.

But remember that is what you come for, Clarise. So just be brave, man. Tell her. Watch how the woman smile hurting-up her face now. Is time . . . Hurry! Tell her! Talk fast!

Is lean Clarise leaning over the desk now, close to the woman ears and saying slow slow:

"My name is Clarise, and I doesn't have greencard."

"What did you say? I'm sorry, I didn't understand what you just said. Your name is Clarise and what?"

Ow Lawd! She want me to shout? But I don't want no ears besides hers to hear my business in here, I don't know how much chickenhawk it have in this room. And is *why* she don't understand me? Ain't every word I say is a *English* word? Is not English America does talk? Or them have they own language?

My name is Clarise and I *doesn't* . . . *have* . . . *greencard*? Is not English that?

Is de language then? Is de Guyanese accent or what? Is de not-understanding-me Mavis talking bout? But I know I talk plain enough in her ears . . . No, man! Is not no understand she not understanding or

hear she not hearing me. She mustbe playing-de-ass
with sheself.
Lemme see again?
And is lean Clarise leaning forward again and say
she saying the same thing in the woman ears:
"I say: My name is Clarise, and I doesn't have
greencard!"
Ow, Clarise, is why you had to tell her justso again?
You coulda change-it-up a lil . . . But why? Is why I
have to change-up what I mean before it reach my
mouth?
Eh-eh! But watch! Hear! Look!
Is magic!
Is the woman taking-off like acourri.
"What's that? *A dozen of you have green cards?*
Well!"
Eh-eh! Justso?
Is the pain vanishing like magic from the lady smile
and her face loose-up in a broad-smile.
"Ha-ha-ha-ha!"
Is a big-laugh she bust-out.
Eh-eh!
Is laugh she laughing? Eh-eh! F'what? Is what is
she case? What so funny bout what I say? Mustbe de
honesty. Mustbe too much f'she.
"Bring them! Bring them! Where *are* they? A *dozen*
of you have green cards?"
Well what is this at all? Is talk the hardface woman
talking to Clarise and . . .
Aye aye aye. Is sigh Clarise sighing in her mind.
Lawd! Is why? Is how come people don't understand
one-another so, eh? Is what she saying to me now? She
have me confuse . . . But who you going blame? Is all
your fault, Clarise. You should try a lil harder cause is
not you want de job? Try Clarise. Try try try! Try lil bit.

Clarise still talking to herself:

Yes, I know. I know I know. But ow! Feel for me, nuh? Is not me self too? Is me, Clarise . . . And is who is Clarise? *That* is de question!

Is how I *am*. Is how I *look*. Is how I *feel* right now. Tired tired tired. Disgust! Vex!

Is how I miss my man and how I want him back that's why I have to be passing through all this . . . this . . . And if I don't find him, is what I going do?

Is how my money running out and I want work but nobody won't give me any that mean anything to my problems and I don't know what to do. Is how I miss my children and my mother and de coconut-tree side my kitchenwindow, my butcher that does tease me in de market, and my neighbor Miz Goring calling out and gaffing me while we cooking pon-a-day.

Is me how I does talk to m'self in this godforsaken country bout all these things that distressing my mind. Cause my life in pieces. Is what I going do? Is how I going get-back-whole again?

Is me just *here, now,* who tell her what I had to say just like I say it in my head, in my *mind,* not true?

Is not me how I talking in my head?

Is who she really want to talk to? Me? Or . . .

She want to talk to de person who want de *job,* Clarise, and that person have to talk to her how she want to hear. Is who want de job, Clarise? Not you?

Yes, is me want de job. Is me is me is me is me Clarise want de job. I want it baaaad!

"You *did* say a dozen of you have green cards, didn't you?"

Is the woman with her face light up like Christmas-tree asking again bout the dozen of them with . . .

"Greencards? Yes, ma'am!"

Eh-eh!

Is Clarise pulling out Mavis greencard and shoving it under the woman nose:

"And look mine here. Watch good, look! See? Is me. Is me. Is only cause I seeing better days in those days . . . my younger days. But just look at de hairstyle good, and watch me!"

"But this says —"

"Mavis Drakes? Yes yes! But look good at it. Look good! Clarise is only my *call* name. Mavis is my *real* name. Is Mavis I name."

"Wellll . . . okay. Here, take this form and fill it out. There're pens over there. We have an opening right now on Fifty-ninth Street. You take the Lexington Avenue line to . . ." And the woman give Clarise the directions to the job, right down to the apartment number and the lady name: Miz Bradford.

Clarise take a seat in the corner where the woman point, at a desk where nobody not nearby. She sit quiet a lil to catch herself and laugh over in her mind what happen.

Eh-eh!

Well *she* proper get jubilant when she think that a dozen o' we got greencard. I wonder is what? Mustbe de money? I wonder is how much she is get for one o' we.

Hmm . . . Is that! Ha-ha ha-ha! She think she have a dozen *slaves* from Guyana. She counting her profits already. Ha! Clarise chile, like you *score*. This round here is for you.

Ha-ha-ha-he-he! Ow Lawd! Don't make I laugh like de song:

> De upper-class laugh: hee-hee-hee
> De middle-class laugh: ho-ho-ho
> But when it come to de *ordinary* class . . .

Ow Lawd! Me belly! I-going-die-oie! This here a belly-laugh, yes! Clarise say. Talking and laughing to herself till she pick up the form she suppose to full-up and she watch it.

Eh-eh!

Is *all* them questions like they have tricks in them and she fraid to start. First trick is she have to write Mavis name instead of hers. Then she have to write Mavis life.

But as soon as she look at the form like her mind turn a complete blank. She can't remember how Mavis tell her to full-up the forms. She can't even see the questions good. Cause she not looking she just boxing her brains trying to remember all what she learn-up with Mavis so she would know when time like this come.

Steewpps!

I tell she I doesn't have greencard and she going hear *a dozen of we have greencards.* Well, let she take me first.

Is I name Mavis Drakes and I'm the first one with greencard . . .

But who de hell is Mavis Drakes?

Clarise watch the form in her hand and she start to laugh again. Clarise laughing lil easy till she find she can't keep the laugh down because it want to burst out her mouth from her belly. She holding it back and the tears rolling out her eyes. Clarise shaking and crying and a lady look round with a Jamaican voice:

"You all right there, miss?"

Clarise can't answer her cause she shaking and laughing and crying and feeling in her bag for a piece of toiletpaper she have there to wipe her eyes!

She raise her hand to thank the woman. She get up from the chair at the desk in the corner and she walk up to the woman with the hardface at the front desk who like everybody else in the room want to laugh too with Clarise but they ain't too sure if Clarise laughing or she crying cause Clarise ain't too sure herself.

Clarise put the form down pon the desk and start to walk to the door.

"Hey! You didn't fill out the form! And what about the others?"

Clarise have to get outside fast, then.

Okay, Clarise, catch y'self now. *Catch yourself quick!* Is what you going do now?

I doanno I doanno, I don't know, Lawd!

Think, Clarise. Think! You have one last address on the paper. But you see him already and he tell you to call him next week. He say he still interviewing. You can't go. What you going *do*, Clarise.

Oh! Is what she say that woman name? Miz Bradford? De Lexington Avenue line? I wonder how you could go by de busway?

Forget de bus, Clarise, just go how hardface woman tell you to go. Go justso . . .

Clarise heart beating buddupbuddupbuddup on the train where she sit up stiff and staring one place like everybody else staring into space. But Clarise eyes fasten pon a advertisement and she reading it over and over and over again: "NOTICIAS DEL MUNDO: LO INUITA A JUGAR Y GANAR CON. CRAZY CASH! PREMIO MAYOR $10,000" cause she don't want to think what going happen if her story don't work. She plan to get the work first then tell the woman *after* she get it that the agency didn't send her in truth. So she reading that one advertisement over and over in her nervousness: "CRAZY CASH . . . $10,000 . . ."

When she reach the apartment she see a man

wearing nice watchman clothes, serge-suit with gold braid pon it and on his hat, too. He ask her is who she come to. When she say, "Miz Bradford," he say, "Is she expecting you?"

Clarise say, "I don't know if de agency tell her yet but I —"

"I'll call her and find out," the man say. "Please wait here."

As soon as the watchman walk away a body grab Clarise hand.

"Chile? You is a Guyanese, eh?"

Clarise see a face she don't recognize but it look like it come from home. "Yes," she say before she could stop herself. "You?"

"Yes, chile, yes. Y'see? Is God! Is *he* make I meet you so to warn you. Is that Bradfordwoman you going work for?"

"Yes . . . I . . . ."

"Y'have children?"

"Yes, but —"

"Chile? Lemme tell you something! That woman don't have no *heart*. I working for *ten years* in this country and I *never see nobody like she*. Is *my* job you going get. And if I was you I'd a-walk right outa here and left she before I ever *see* she. It don't matter *what* happening in your life . . . If you or your chile there pon dying or it snowing-and-storming and you come and tell that woman you ain't come to work in time cause? She *still* going tell you bout how you *interfere* with her plans for her bridgeparty or some stupidness so. I had to tell she this mawning that when de day come? All *she* have to look after is two bubby and a cat! But *I* have *two children* depending pon me in this place and —"

106

"Mrs. Bradford says I should see you out," the watchman say to the woman.

"You don't put your hand pon me, mister. Not a *finger* you is to lay pon me! I talking to this lady here!"

"Mrs. Bradford says you can go up, miss . . ." the man say to Clarise. "Take that elevator over there to the eighth floor. You have the number? Good.

"You, miss, will have to leave."

"Look! You kiss-my-ass, hear? Is what your name, chile?"

"Clarise."

"I name Rosalie . . . You going? You going work for that ole bitch?"

"Yes, I have to go. I want work," Clarise say.

"All right, but I *warning* you . . ." Rosalie say.

"Please . . ." the watchman say.

"But is what is wrong with this *auntie*-man, eh? You can't see I going? I getting out this damn place here before allyuh make me commit myself in this country. Clarise chile, I gone. All I can do is wish you luck with she, cause she . . ."

Clarise tell her goodbye quick and head for the elevator the watchman show her. She go in and press eight.

When she get off at the eighth floor she find herself in a square box with doors all round and a nice black-iron table with curly legs and fancy working and a big-mirror in a frame just like the table over it. She watch her face.

You looking good, Clarise, don't mind you tired, once you don't let it get to your face. You going all right. Don't let this place get to your head, chile. Don't let them bassidy you. Look for eight F . . . Look, it here. Now ring de bell.

Rinnng!

"Who's there?"

"Clarise, from de agency!"

The door open and Clarise see a ole lady with a stick and a face full of lines.

I wonder what put them lines there? Clarise say to herself. Mustbe Rosalie cause some. But if she living in big-house and can afford to hire me, what is her story? How come she have all them? Mustbe Rosalie . . .

"What's your name?"

"Clarise Cumberbatch," Clarise tell the woman. Then she say in her mind: Ow, but this is a *nice* house . . .

"And where are you from, Clarise?"

"Guyan —"

Before Clarise could catch herself or before she could finish saying *Guyana* the woman say:

"*Guyana?* Oh my God! No! No, no, no! Not again. Not *another* one. I must call the agency and tell them, no more of *you people from Guyana*."

SLAM!

Eh-eh!

But is how all o' we people from Guyana get involved in she story with Rosalie? Just cause *one* o' we working f'she vex she? Is justso she going condemn a whole-nation-o'-people? *Steewpps!* Some people could properly constipate!

And you? You still in de same boat, Clarise. You left same place.

Now what?

Home! By bus and shortcut! Home! This day done!

Clarise start walking fast cross the road to the alley. But it dark and she frighten so she go up to a woman who heading to the alley too.

"Miss-lady!" Clarise call out. "Miss-lady, scuse me asking, but you taking de shortcut through here?"

"Yes . . . Why?"

"You won't mind if I walk along with you, please? . . . They tell me that after dark I mustn't walk here alone cause you don't know *what* could happen . . ."

"*I* know what could happen. Some *horny bastard* could jump on you and get off on you in that old building over there. That's what could happen."

"What you say, miss?"

"*Rape*, sister! I'm talkin' bout rape. I'm sayin' you could get raped here *any*time, not just after dark. And robbed . . . it's the same anyway . . . Other day this dude was carrying his baby? Got held up by some *punk* teenager who asked him for his money. Guy's got his kid in his arms and he ain't safe. He gave that punk his money and *still* got shot. Can you *dig* that?

"Then this friend of mine she got it in the basement, you know? In the laundry room. Two dudes jumped on her. Couldn't make up their cott'n pickin' minds who'd go first. She tried to run away and WHAM! She never knew who won the argument. Happened three weeks ago. She's *still* in hospital."

"But why, miss lady? Why?"

"Hell, cause men are *sick*, that's why! And this is America. Where you from, sister? Africa? Anyway, I got me this *lugar* in my pocket . . . see? And if anyone messes with me I'm gonna let him have it *right where he lives!* You should get yourself one of these things, sister. You can't be without one — not in New York, at least."

Clarise watch the lil gun the woman pull out her pocket, then she watch that lady again with her eye full of wonder. Then her eye catch a young girl look like eighteen year old or so, leaning gainst a door on the steps of a burn-out apartment building. That girl look sick. Like she want to fall down. She swaying like coconut-tree in the wind.

Clarise cry out!

"Ohhh, she going fall down! Like she sick! Lehwe see if we could help her!"

"Who? Her? Help her? How you gonna do that? You got a fix to give her? She's waitin' for her *fix*, that's all. C'mon, don't linger here, sister . . .

"What's this? A picture? What . . . who's he? Who is this dude?" the woman say, taking Harold picture from Clarise and looking at it before giving it back.

"You know him?"

"Hell no! I don't care to know him either. What's his story?"

"He my husband. I looking for him."

"Why? He lost or something?"

"Yes, he leave home and I don't know where he is."

"Well let him go, sister. What you looking for that man for? Ain't you had enough of that kind of heartbreak? Sheeee-it! What's your name?" the woman ask Clarise.

"Clarise . . ."

"Look, Clarise, sister, my name's Ellie and I'm gay. I don't belong to no movement. I don't belong to no group. I don't want to cut off no man's balls. But take my advice, forget this Harold creature. He ain't worth it!

"Here's where I get off. You want to talk to me anytime, come on up, apartment seven C. Seventh floor. Just call before you come, that's all. Name is Ellie Plate. Look in the New York directory under P. Be glad to talk with you, *anytime* . . ."

Nine

Clar? Clarise, ole girl? Is how you making out?

Me? I here, I here . . . nigger-belly backra-mouth . . . hungry-like-a-nigger, but . . . talking-like-a-backra . . . confuse, poor, vex! It looking like nothing ain't working and I run-outa-luck.

I want to go home. But how? F'what? Dying to find a proper job. But where? Nobody don't care, and I don't know nobody . . . only Mavis, Mr. Blades, Bella . . .

No time no time no money to nice-up m'self! Go-out-and-shout! F'lil joy . . .

And like *thing biting me* all over my body. Or must-be nerves . . . I got nerves? . . . I just doanno what-to-do with all this dread? Sometimes I does feel as if I going outa my head.

But I talking to m'self!

Steady!

Cause I ain't ready to join them people-out-there . . . though, y'know what? That is maybe a way to live. When you turn madwoman in Guyana? De baglady in America? You could pack up your clothes in a crocus-bag, that is your bed. And don't forget to tie-up your head. Then you leave your home (if y'have one) and all o' de dread . . .

Is going be no more hair f'comb schoolclothes f'wash, breakfast f'cook . . . When you hungry you could always steal . . . a banana-orange-pine or pawpaw from somebody tray and run away. Don't pay . . . People who see? Would just glad to say *She? Left she! She mad!* But over here so? Ohhh nooooo! When you reach that stage you playing-with-more-trouble-than-your-age . . .

Me? I ain't ready f'that. I does have to talk to m'self . . . and I know is what:

> is de nuff-nuff people
> pon de streets
> pon de train
> pon de bus
> everyday!
> From Sunday-to-Sunday
> pon a Good Friday, too . . .

And this snowing, y'know? No matter how it pouring, you still have to get-up-and-going . . . Not like how we does shelter from de rain . . .

Is too much . . .

PAIN!

This place ain't kind pon de mind . . .

And why they does nasty-up de place so? I'll never know. Watch de streets with de rubbish. Watch de trains . . . and de subway? All that ugly writing-up, dirty-up dirty-up! F'what? Just to smear-up? What they call it? *Graf-eat-he* or something?

It got de place looking too stinking. It does sicken my stomach to come down here to catch de train. But what y'going do?

Lot 19
Middlewalk Dam
Beterverwagting
East Coast Domerara

Dear Mummy,

I love you. Do you notice the more you miss people the more you love them? Well I love you and Auntie Mavis and Daddy too. Regardless. I am fine. Is it nice there? Is it snowing? How fat are you? Did you really buy boxing gloves for us?

Mummy, Clarence ran away from home. He wanted to go in the bush and Granny said no so he disappeared for a whole week. Granny said she was not going to worry but everybody could see she was worrying about what you would say. Only yesterday Clarence told me why he did it (I have to give him my sugar cake first). Do you remember that Amerindian boy Ignatius? Clarence said Ignatius is not coming back to school. He said he can make up to five or six pennyweights of gold a day. He is in a place name Konawaruk. Clarence told Mrs. Barr that Ignatius is not going to school anymore because he can count already.

Clarence wanted to go back with him to water-dog for gold at Konawaruk. But he is back home now and everything is okay I think.

Miss says to tell you I am doing well in school. She says Clarence is a bright boy but he won't settle down. Granny says to send her some hair dye in the barrel. She says not red, send black. Miss

113

Goring says to tell her daughter to write her and send some milk and oil for her. Did she get her baby? Is it a boy or a girl? Christie was a model at her school fair but she was going too fast. Mummy, please, please, please. Please come home. We all miss you, especially me. Please bring a video when you are coming.

Love,
Eunice

XXXXXXXXXXXXXXXXXOOOOOOOOOOOOOOOOO
    Kisses   *Hugs*

P.S. Bring Daddy and Auntie Mavis too with you. — E.C.

"Owww! I ain't even get chance to see Miz Goring grandson . . ." Clarise moan and close up the letter.

"What is the news?" Mavis ask.

"Clarence want to go in de gold bush. Eunice doing well in school and they expecting de barrel I promise to send."

"But Clarise, they don't know what you passing through? You didn't tell them?"

"Mavis, I write but like I couldn't bring m'self to tell them. I now know what does happen. Is not that people who come does talk lies bout de life here and encourage others to come. No! They does just *forget* to tell everything and leave people with they nice dreams. Cause when you punishing in a place is nice to know it have somewhere to escape to if you get through. Is nice to have a dream . . . And that is what America is, a dream — till you wake up in *this damn nightmare*."

"Hmmm!" Mavis groan. "Okay okay Clarise, don't start again. Tell me, she say anything bout her father?"

"Yes . . . Look man! Take it, you read de letter."

Mavis take the letter from Clarise and read it. Then she bust-out:

"Bring *who*? ME? Clarise, you better tell that chile that if she want to see me she have to come to America. But at least she know where to find me. You better get her accustom to de fact that her father done *mystic* for good. He into he own *vibrations* . . . But is what is this waterdawg thing with Clarence?"

"Is in de Essequibo, I see it work. In de dry-season when riverwater low? If you don't have dredge to do riverwork and you don't have pump to do landwork you can go in de creeks and waterdawg with a facemask.

"Chile? I see that thing when I was a young woman in that same Konawaruk area where B.G. Consolidated Goldmine was. They would go down, dive for as long as they could stay down with de facemask and a canvas-bag or something to collect de gravel from five, six, ten feet under water. Then that gravel? They wash it out in a batelle: first de big-stones, then de lil pebbles, then sand, till they come to de black-sand and then de gold resting in de thimble, de bottom of de batelle . . .

"Chile? I see women in Tumatumari living under two zinc-sheet or a piece tarpaulin working the tail-race or de black-sand de dredges leave. If you see them women kneading de clay like bread, and taking out de *living thing*. Mavis! De gold! *De-bright-yellow-gold*. But is plenty work and it ain't easy. Is hard work. Is grind. But y'could make! Y'could make! You could make a lil thing every day. You could live —"

"Not me! Lemme stay right *here*," Mavis say.

"Yeah! Eh-eh! You stay here, Mavis, in de cold-and-de-snow-and-de-subway-jam . . . Is what de man say in that song? *"All them West Indians jamming down in de subway?"* Is now I know what he mean. We squeeze-up like sardine. Is all o' we jamming down. At least home in de bush you could stop work in de afternoon and listen to de song of de waterfall and watch de moon go down over de mountain or something. Them-two is good company, de river and de mountain. Me? If I coulda seen my way? I woulda go straight back home to de bush and stay. And y'would have to get *crowbar* to move me . . .

"Mavis, I doanno I doanno. I don't know! If it have a thing name *better punishment*? I would say it better to punish so — home . . . Not worry with Georgetown. That coastland? That is *dread,* like de Rastaman does say. But de bush? If you have de guts, Mavis? That is *I-ree!* And you could make! You could make a living . . ."

Clarise like she gone off dreaming again. Mavis staring at her with her mouth open, say:

"Clarise, you not telling me y'would seriously think bout . . ."

"Why not, Mavis? I been in de bush already, you know? My father before me . . . my *grandfather* was a pork-knocker, y'know? He did know all them people like Sultan and Tengar . . ."

"Who is Sultan and Tengar?"

"Eh-eh, Mavis? You sure you born same place with me? Like you not know bout ole-time bushman and bushstory?"

"No, I did too busy punishing to hear story. From de time I *born* life was a punishment. They tell me Independence come and as de man say in de song, 'Is a day of excitement!' Things going change. But Independence come and gone and poor Mavis still punishing. I never know my daddy . . . And when I was ten years old my mammie take a ignar of a man who use to abuse my body and tell me if I tell her? What-and what he ain't going do to me, and she too . . . So when you see God help me and I get through to come here? I ring m'ears. I wipe de dust, m'dear. I wipe de dust off my feet . . . But don't worry with Sultan and Tengar or whatever. Tell me, when you been in de bush, Clarise?"

"Was a long time ago, man, and to tell you I going have to talk bout —"

"Harold Cumberbatch! God-Lawd! No! Don't tell me, then. *Please* don't tell me. Goodnight, Clarise, I gone to bed."

"Goodnight, Mavis . . ."

"Clarise? You sleeping?"

"No, Mavis, what?"

"You don't miss having your lil *thing*?"

"How you mean, Mavis? Is three years, y'know? You ain't see how much limewater I drinking to keep down my nature?"

"*Steewpps!* Clarise, you lie, not three years! You couldn't last three years pon limewater. That don't help with a thing."

"Don't tell me, Mavis, ask me, please, cause you have Mr. Blades."

"*Steewpps!* He don't keep down my nature. *He* can't keep down my nature."

"Well, whoever else with he . . . Is not my business . . ."

"You want me tell you who else does really keep down —"

"No, Mavis! No!" Clarise shout-out, but Mavis laugh and go on talking:

"Y'see, every Saturday-weekend? When you baby-sitting and I gone —"

Clarise cut Mavis.

"I thought you was going to Mr. Blades all this time!"

"*Steewpps!* Which-side!" Mavis say: "Y'know is who I —"

"No! Jesus-Lawd-I-ask-for-mercy! Mavis, don't tell me, please. I know that man, I like him — Mr. Blades, I mean — I don't want to have no guilty news."

"All right, all right all right! Sleep, Clarise. Rest easy. I ain't going tell you . . . But is why you protecting Blades so? I got to watch y'all. Every time he come he asking for you and you so concern bout he. You not planning to take my good-living away from me, eh, friend?"

Rinnng!

"Don't answer it! No, too-besides answer it. Might be Bella calling again. Y'know how she is a after-hours caller . . ."

Rinnng!

"It nearer to you outside there, Clarise, I ain't able to move. Only if is Bella you must call me."

Clarise go and pick up the phone.

"Hello?"

"Mavis, doll, how y'doing? Guess what? I'm lying here thinking —"

"Is not Mavis. Is Clarise. Is who? Miz Bella?"

"Ohhh . . . Clarise, dollbaby! You still there? How ya doing, doll?"

"I all right, Miz Bella. How you?"

"Well, doll, I'm as busy as a spider spinning a web. Tell me, why don't I ever see you at our group meetings? Tell Mavis to bring you along one weekend. Hell, doll, you can't spend all your time looking for that man and lose yourself, know what I mean?"

"Yes, Miz Bella, I will come if Mavis bring me. But really, de weekends is de only time I have to wash a lil clothes and shop for a lil things I have to take home, or catch my hand if I find a lil babysitting . . ."

"Oh, you going *home* soon?"

"Maybe not soon, but I going home, Miz Bella. I am going home."

"Hummm hummm hummm! Doll, doll, doll. Doll-baby! You gonna have to get that dude off your mind. You sound so sad each time I talk to you, you seem so blue each time I see you. You gonna have to come and sit a little with the sisters and let's talk. Oh, we have a lot of fun, but we do be serious most of the time. Our latest project is trying to get Mavis's hands out of the pocket of that dude Blades so she could truly, seriously, get him out of her system. Know what I mean?"

"Dollbaby? You listen to me, hear? It's the *economic system*. You look careful at all our troubles in the world, see if it doesn't point right to the economic system. A woman don't need no man to take care of her, unless he really cares for her. She don't need no man to destroy her mind, make her think she's less than she's worth. But if she's got to depend on him . . . hummm hummm hummm! Now, take me. I once had a husband . . . You know that?"

"No, Miz Bella. I don't know your —"

"Oh, you mean Mavis didn't tell you about me? But, hey! Don't you keep referring to me as Miss Bella. I'm just plain Bella, your sistah . . . Saaay! Where's my girl? Let me talk to her . . ."

Is what, Clarise?
Is what is what is what?
I doanno . . .
mustbe de . . .
WHEEL OF FORTUNE
mustbe de

119

JOKER
that
IS WILD
or
the
PRICE that
IS RIGHT.
Mussee people steady
eating . . .
then taking medicine
for
IN-DI-GES-TION!
and asking if they could discuss
(scuse me please)
DIARRHEA
with yuh . . .
Mussee
the Muppets:
    . . . every head would be held up high
    there'd be sunshine in everyone's sky
    if the day ever dawned
    when
    WE
    ruled the world.

Oh, but *look!* Those Muppets are such *cute* little puppets, eh?

Ten

"Clarise, the phone is for you," Mavis calling out.

"Is who?" Clarise ask her.

"Is how I going know? You have more calls than a doctor. Somebody else mustbe see Harold and want you waste time-and-money to go Long Island or New Jersey again. Lemme hand it to you, you got patience. You *really* got patience. All o' them who calling ain't got nothing-to-do. They idle, and you —"

"Is a woman, Mavis?"

"It sound so, but y'is never to know."

"Mustbe Miz Mann. Lawd!"

"She is de *most* idle of them all. Is how much places she send you already?"

"Mavis, please, be a friend . . ."

"Not me! Last time I was a friend and take that on

for you? That woman keep me *one hour* pon de phone telling me *exactly* how she harass some poor man in a three-piece-suit working pon Madison Avenue and insisting that he have to be Harold cause she have de picture you give her resemble him. This time I know to my bosom that de only tip you should follow up on Harold Cumberbatch is if you hear bout somebody who always hanging out by de OTB, which is de last place I did see him."

"Mavis, is what Harold ever do you, eh?"

"He got my friend bassidy, is *that* what he do me. And he is a whore. If you see he, tell he I Mavis say so! Now, go! Quick! De lady on de phone."

"I ain't going."

"Is why you stay so? Is how you could give people lead-up so and now you backing out?"

"I tired!"

"Well, stop!"

"I thinking bout it. I can't look for a good work and look for Harold Cumberbatch same time. It drying my pocket and my time and my energy . . . *Steewpps!*"

"Is *now* I hearing sense. Go and answer de phone, though."

"No!"

"Clarise, I say, *answer de phone!*"

"I say no, Mavis!"

"Well, let it rest right there. She will go away when she tired."

"Okay!"

Is whole summer Clarise searching for Harold. Sometimes she didn't even know she going on wild-goose-chase cause some of the people who sending her just like Miz Mann. Miz Mann is a nice lil ole woman she meet-up one day sitting on a bench in the park. If Clarise did only know what she was putting herself into she woulda never breathe a word to that woman. But that time all she could think bout was finding her husband and when she go sit down on the parkbench near her that day, just to rest-and-think? Miz Mann give her such a pleasant goodafternoon and say, "Nice day today, isn't it? Reminds me of a New England autumn. Where are you from?" that Clarise couldn't stop herself from talking.

And is so one thing lead to another and Clarise end up telling that lady her whole story bout Harold. And every week since then Miz Mann finding Harold for Clarise. She take on the problem like if is her own.

One day when Clarise come home to hear from Mavis that Miz Mann find Harold again? Mavis say:

"She say *this* time she know it *have* to be he, cause he look guilty. She say he obviously doing well for heself cause she follow him right up to his office, but like he using another name. She say you must go to this address and ask for —

"Clarise," Mavis say suddenly, "Harold not going be working at this address. This is de business district. That woman head ain't good! She even want we go with she to some antinuclear demonstration in Washington. She tell me she going pay de passage f'we: bring your friends, she say, cause they need people to protest de building of some *shit* somewhere . . . But too-besides, it take one *nut* to recruit another-one. I tell you, you *proper* got she pon Harold case.

"But you know what happen to that lady? Is de same thing, I tell you. Is de all-o'-we-look-alike syndrome. So when every blackman going along bout he business in de streets? Miz lady stopping him to ask him if his name Harold Cumberbatch and when he tell her no? He can't know that that ole crone feel that he looking guilty when he say so. If he *irritate* it must be looking like guilt to her. This time she following de man to his workplace and she got detective agency on he case too. Ha! Allyuh too comical," Mavis say that day.

Now she saying:

"*Clarise!* The phone again! Is you set up de woman! She working for you! Go!"

"No, she not working for me. And too-besides, she working too hard. Is true what you say, she too idle and she confusing me. Is *ten* places I been already. Is she send me to *six*. All is wild-goose-chase. No! When she tired she going hang up de phone. I tired. She too kind. If kindness is her mission in life let she try with somebody else. She only putting me in more confusion than my life have already. No! No! Please, no more, no!"

"Ow Lawd! Clarise, when you come to this country? You were a *reasonable person*. Y'was lil kankawa, yes, but more reasonable. You woulda never let somebody stay pon de phone waiting pon you like that."

"I know, this country could change people. I changing . . . Mavis?"

"Yes, Clarise? Ow God, Clarise, is why you like to wait till I sleeping? What is it, Clarise?"

"Mavis, what is gay?"

"Clarise, is who you been talking to?"

"Don't worry with that, is a long story and you say y'want to sleep. Just tell me, what is gay?"

"Gay is when a man and a man or a woman and another woman *friendsing* with one-another. Is who tell you bout gay?"

"Is like working *sodomite*?"

"Yes, but Clarise, don't say that Guyana-foolishness! It sound bad . . . But is who tell you?"

"A woman I meet a day, de other-day through de shortcut."

"What she say to —"

"And what is a male sov . . . shovinist pig?" Clarise ask.

"A man who think he is God self! And he don't give two *shits* bout what a woman have in her head bout herself. Only since I come here I learn to understand they meaning. All de time I use to say leave them alone, is so they stay. They can't change. But y'see now? A male chauvinist pig is . . . is a *Harold Cumberbatch!*"

"No . . . I doanno is so Harold stay, Mavis. He ain't really stay so. If he think he is God is why he running so? God don't run away from nobody so. God does wait for you to catch up, God does stay to show you de way. No! No no no, Mavis. Harold ain't stay so. He in some kind of trouble, is all. He in trouble.

"And you know what? Is his mother. Is she got he so. Is she spoil he so he don't know how to hold lil strain, to brace gainst it. But if you tell her that? Y'know what? She going say is me, is *me* who do he so. Y'know her? She going start giving you chapter-and-verse from Genesis to Revelation as to how is *me* who spoil-up she one-boy-chile. She ain't going tell you is she. Is *she*, though. Is his mother and she navel-string. Is she who spoil he."

Clarise lie down quiet lil bit, then:

"Mavis?"

"Ow, Clarise, what?"

"What is a *fix*?"

"What I in right now with you, Clarise. I want to sleep and you like you ain't intend to shut up. That is a *fix*, Clarise."

"Man, Mavis, you joking, man."

Clarise fretting. She stewpsing and fretting cause she trying to light her coalpot but the coals wet. The coalsman wet-up the coals again.

Steewpps! Is how much money he going make with a lil extra wet-coals-weight, eh? God Lawd! People properly sinning they soul to live now-a-these-days. I tell you! Is *every*body thiefing and robbing-up they mattie. Nobody ain't got conscience no more. Like cockroach eat out everybody conscience. *Steewpps!*

Clarise sucking-up her teeth and cooking. Breakfast late. The coalpot slow cause the coals wet. If she been in the bush she coulda look for a mora-tree with a hole in it and throw it down left it to burn, pray for de rain to come slow-up de fire. And next thing y'know is some nice solid coals. Cook quick!

Eh-eh! Is what is that?

Is a big-commotion outside. Clarise run quick to the window. She look down the road. Is everybody running to the bauxite hill.

Something happen!

Clarise forget her pot on the fire, she forget to put on the shoe, even, and is take she take off behind the people, till she get to the hill.

When she reach the top, she stop, look in.

Is the children, her two among them, staring up at her with they eyes round and frighten and they hands stretching up begging to come out.

But is how they fall in there?

"Harold! Harold! Harold!" Clarise running back down the hill bawling.

"Harold, come quick!"

But Harold ain't come home yet.

Is you alone got to get them children out that hole, girl, cause people only staring and ringing they fingers and screaming. Nobody ain't doing nothing . . .

Clarise running and screaming, running and screaming:

"Eunice! Clarence! Mammie coming!"

She hear a voice behind her. She turn and say, "Harold! Come! Come quick!"

"What happen, Clarise?"

"Is Clarence and Eunice. They fall in de bauxite hole."

"And is where you been, Clarise?"

"Cooking de food . . ."

"You mean you been talking stupidness with Miz Goring insteada keeping your eye pon your children."

"When you working is what else you does seeing and doing, Harold?"

"But I *working,* Clarise, I have to go to work whole day. You home."

"Eunice! Clarence! Hold on hold on hold on m'children . . . Mammie . . . is . . . COMING! . . . She is JUMPING IN! . . . WAIT FOR MEEEEE . . . Ahhhhh . . . !"

"CLAR-ISE!"

Is Mavis shout out Clarise name so.

"Yes yes yes?" Clarise say.

"Wake up! You screaming in your sleep."

"Yes, must be dream I was dreaming . . . that de children fall in de bauxite hole and me and Harold standing-up pon de overburden, blaming one-another. Just blaming one-another . . ."

Is Mavis still on the telephone:

"Bella? I ain't tell you? This lady, my friend Clarise, is MAD! That's why I ain't bringing her to no woman's meeting to let her head get mess up more. My sister here pon her *own* vibration. She don't need no different bration. No! Not so! No way!

"Y'all got me cause I did ready-like-Freddie when I come here. But Clarise, here, she going *never* ready.

She love Harold Cumberbatch like how-hawg-love-shit! No matter what he do she. And if is not he? Going be some other man going get she in-she-place . . . She don't want no *meeting* to describe her head. She got a head all by sheself, all she own! It would break her po' lil heart if we really explain to she *exactly* what is a male chauvinist pig . . . Okay . . . Goodnight, Bella . . . What? If you remember, call me again. Bye.

"You sleeping, Clarise?"

"No, Mavis."

"Bella want you to come to de women's meeting, but I tell her —"

"I hear you, Mavis, you right . . ."

"Tell me bout de dream."

"That is all to it. We, me and Harold, stand-up pon de overburden, y'know? De hill make from earth come out de bauxite hole and we blaming one-another cause de children fall in . . .

"But y'know what? That dream remind me bout something else, and that was not a dream . . . that was no dream at all. I didn't dream that one. That one happen in truth . . .

"My time did nearly meet to-get-baby, Clarence. I was cooking breakfast one day when I hear this big-commotion outside. I look through de window and see like is de whole village running running running. I didn't know was what, but I just decide to follow everybody and I throw off my apron, turn off de stove, slip on my slippers, and dash out de house. Is de *whole* village running that day to de public-road."

"Is what did happen?" Mavis ask.

"They kill ole-man Sampson and his wife Miz Evadne a-back Buxton Village. Remember them-two nice ole people? Use to plant provisions, raise they children nice? One of de boys in America turning doctor, and de girl is schoolteacher at Bladenhall Multilateral?

"No! I say that day. No no no no NO! Is who could *kill* them-two people who never trouble anybody? Is who coulda do a thing like that?

"What? That day? Is so de whole area running to Buxton back-dam alongside de Middlewalk Dam where of course de whole of Buxton self turn out too. People was running coming all from up de seawall side. Is everybody hear de news . . . Is everybody leave stove, stop pot, forget to put on clean clothes, shoes, or even pee! Is so all o' we going running down de road. And me with me big-belly, too . . . we all want to see if is true somebody kill Mr. Sampson and Miz Evadne f'true. Y'does have to *see* story to believe it, not so?

"Anyway, when we reach de back-dam? I force my way through de crowd. Funeral-parlor-man was already there, but I still couldn't believe. Then I get near enough to see something pon de ground cover-up with tarpaulin. I see nearby where Mr. Sampson and Miz Evadne have some baskets full with de provisions they reap from de farm. They did already pack up to leave de back-dam and y'could see de mud still fresh pon de eddoe, de cassava and sweetpotato, y'know? All ready to put in de canoe and go . . .

"Ohhh!" Clarise hold her head and cry out with pain from her memory.

"Was had some nice bunches of green plantains, too, and they were even preparing to cook some metagee cause de squeeze-out coconut-couscous was sitting right there in a bowl, de milk in a pot, de provisions peel-up and put in some water to wash, and some dawgs was having a good time with some saltfish . . .

"Ow Lawd! Is who coulda do such-a-thing? I say

to m'self, and I move up closer, not just cause I fast, but I just *had to see* Miz Evadne face for de last . . .

"And just then de funeral-parlor-man throw back de tarpaulin, de crowd press forward to see, and we all scream out together . . . Cause where we expecting to see Mr. Sampson and Miz Evadne face? Was nothing but a *pulpy mass of flesh-and-blood!*"

"Christ! Yes, I remember that incident . . . but Clarise, I didn't know you see that."

"Just marry and expecting my baby . . . I see that with these two eyes."

"And what happen?" Mavis ask.

"What happen, chile, what happen? Is right there I take-in to get Clarence. They had to hustle quick to get me to de hospital in that *same hearse* come for Mr. Sampson and Miz Evadne. But I ain't reach hospital. Is right in that hearse Clarence born . . ."

"*No!*" Mavis holler. "Clarise, is how I never know this story and I know you so long?"

"Cause I don't talk bout it. That ain't thing to make talk pon. Was only cause de midwife in de village was out de village on her rounds. They had to pack me in de hearse. Was . . .

"Ahhh! God-bless-she-keep-she-safe! Miz Goring again . . . is she who make them put me in de hearse. Cause some them ole people did saying is not a good thing to do. But Miz Goring say, 'When pickney meet time to come, it going come in this world no matter *where* it ready.' She say birth-and-death ain't got no *superstition* them does wait pon. Is we who does visit we foolishness pon them. Since then she was making sense . . .

"And me? Like I get de spirit and catch cumfa, y'know? You ever catch cumfa, Mavis?"

"No."

"Well, you won't understand . . . Was a deep deep blackness I slip into and next thing you know Clarence was screaming inside de hearse hustling all o' we to Georgetown. Was de hospital maternity ward for me, and de mortuary for po' Mr. Sampson and Miz Evadne."

"Geeee!"

Is Mavis say so. And then not another sound till you hear the two of them breathing hard.

Like they fall asleep.

BUP!

Is Clarise land near Clarence in the bauxite hole?

"Is where Eunice?" she ask her son.

"I think she gone to school, Mammie."

"Clarence, I say *where* your sister *is?*"

"She mustbe gone to school already, Mammie."

"But boy, I didn't pass her on de trail and I now walk back from Vansluytman Camp . . . Here, take this. Uncle Gabbo send it for you. He say he going Yowari Island this afternoon and if you want to go you must bring de lil boat with a extra paddle . . .

"Now, you didn't finish telling me . . . where that girl?"

"She mustbe take the shortcut."

"What *shortcut,* Clarence? I don't know no short-cut to teacher —"

"I cut a new track."

"Boy! You only here this short time and already you in that snake bush cutting *sirihi*? Listen to me, too-besides . . . no! *Come with me.* Come now now now now now so. Lehwe go! Bring de paddles, we going *right now!* See that tree? De one yonder by that clump of bush there? Near that big-rock?"

"Which one, Mammie? De tall one?"

"Yes, that *same* one. *That* is de one you use for snakebite. Bahuruda! Is that it name . . . But come, we going look for another-one closer. It have one in a itabu . . . Come . . .

". . . You have to cut de bark, scrape de inside, squeeze out de juice, drink a lil, and squeeze some on de spot . . . Come!

"When we get more settle we going walk de bush together and look for these things. You have a cure for *every sick* in this jungle here. If you go and get yourself a dose of *syphilis* and all? . . ."

"Me? What I going do that for?"

"M'chile, in this world thing like that does *wabuni* f'you, you don't have to go hunt it y'self. And in de most surprising places, too. Mammie will show you . . . And if you was to take a wife? . . ."

"How you mean *if* I —"

"I say *if,* boy, cause I live longer than you, and I know life is a *big* if . . . And if she can't get baby? . . . But all in good time, now we looking for de bahuruda. It was here when me and your daddy was here . . . and look, eh? It still here. If people could only be like . . ."

"Mammie!"

"Yes, Clarence?"

"Daddy ever going come back?"

"When . . . if he find his new life not satisfying him and he hear we making lil gold to save we life . . . Who knows, m'son? Mammie can't say, she ain't God. All I asking you is to keep your mind on what I going try to teach you bout this life that you have here. Believe me son, right here in them mountains and in this river is *all* de life you need and all de *pressure* you could bear is right here too. You can farm your land, catch your fish, eat your food, and get your money out of this same earth, this same river. That is all your mammie can promise you, that as sure as there's a mountain and a river and a sun going down over there every day you going learn to be a responsible man right here.

"And you going learn what it is to care for your own thing, to love, to hold strain . . . Cause it have a thing here like big-water-season could lick you upside-down if you don't know how to brace gainst it."

"Mammie! Mammie, listen! Is a engine! Is a plane?"

"No, boy, is de falls-song! It can make you hear anything you want to hear. Aishalton-plane gone long. Is de falls-song, hear?

"Humm-hmm-hmm-hmm-hmm-hmmmmm! Listen good! Humumumum . . . Sometimes it could sound like a rover when you expecting transpee. Sometimes it sound like a —"

"Symphony orchestra!" Clarence say.

"A what, boy?"

"Music, Mammie, music. Hear? Listen. Hear . . ."

"Yes, Clarence, I hear, but a syn . . ."

"Yes, like a steelband symph —"

"Okay, Clarence, but look now . . . Ain't *that* a sight to see? It name Yukuribi! Is Itami big-side."

"Hmmmmmhmmmmmhmmmmmm . . ."

Ringringringring!

"CLAR-ISE! Lawd! Is madness tonight in this house. *Clarise!* Wake up! De phone ringing and you humming in your sleep. Eh-eh! This here a mass-madness, yes!" Mavis fretting and she pick up the phone.

"Yes? Yes? Bella! Wait a minute, just a second, please . . . Clarise, is what happen to you?"

"Mavis? If I tell you? You ain't going believe me. I dream I jump in de bauxite hole to save my children

133

but this time like it was in de middle of de jungle, and me and —"

"Ohhh God! Bella! I did tell you bout my friend? She *mad!* Clarise mad-as-ass!" Mavis hollering on the phone.

"Y'know what? Clarise *dreaming in serials* and *singing* in her sleep . . . With all my friend worries, she is *singing* in her sleep. Now you tell me if . . ."

Eleven

Clarise!

"Clarise, is that you?

"Over here! I'm over here, Clarise."

"Is who?"

Clarise hearing her name calling and the voice sounding American but she not recognizing it and she waiting to know is who calling her so.

Buddupbupbup! Is not Harold? Suppose? Suppose he voice turn American? Is three years already, y'know.

"Where? Where you?"

Clarise craning her neck over the people at the . . . what they does call it? Peedes-tree-and-crossing? And a woman touch her on her shoulder and say:

"There he is!"

Just near her, only one person away. She could stretch out her hand and touch him?

"Eh! Mr. Blades! Is you? How you do? I so stupid I dreaming-and-gazing and I ain't even look-and-see is you, Mr. Blades! How you do?"

"I'm fine, fine, just fine now that I've seen you, Clarise."

"Me? Oh, I'm glad, Mr. Blades, cause I really happy to see you looking so good. You going by Mavis tonight? She say she ain't see you for a long time."

"Yes, yes, Clarise, but will *you* be there?"

"Me? Oh, um, no, sir. No, y'see, I have to go to a lil prayermeeting."

"What prayer meeting, Clarise? I happen to know you spend your time in the five-and-dime store examining the prices whenever you know I'll be around, or you leave soon after I come. That's why I've stopped calling before I come, and why I don't come so often," Mr. Blades say.

"Tell me, tell me, Clarise. Don't you . . . . can't you do something else? I'd feel a lot better if I knew you were doing something besides roaming through a corner store looking at prices, never being able to buy. Tell me, Clarise, how much do you need to help you through this?"

"I don't want your money, Mr. Blades. I don't take people money justso and I ain't start to sell yet. I don't even know you. And Mavis will know bout it? You will tell her you give me de money?"

"No, Clarise, I won't. I can't."

"But why? Why? Why? If you want to be so kind to me why you can't tell? You don't see something wrong? What is de money for? Not to help me go on searching for a job and for my husband? Without getting on my friend nerves for money and under her foot in her small apartment? So is why you can't tell her?"

136

"It will ruin your friendship with her and Mavis will never forgive me."

"For what, Mr. Blades?"

"Mavis is *greedy*, Clarise, and jealous."

"Greedy? Mavis greedy? No! Never! That is de biggest lie anybody ever tell on a person. Mavis? Greedy?"

"Clarise, Clarise, she's not greedy to you, she *loves* you. She'll give you anything, she's your *real* friend. But she's greedy to everyone else. Think about it, Clarise!"

Come to think about it, is true, y'know? Clarise say to herself, then to Mr. Blades:

"I don't want to talk my friend name with you in de middle of de streets. She helping me through, Mr. Blades. Not even for your money that I need now I going do that. Was really nice talking to you, but I going look for this lil job again . . ."

"Clarise, please, wait, listen . . ."

"I going listen, Mr. Blades, if you could please walk along with me, cause I can't wait. I late! And I not talking my friend name with her man. You is her man, not so?"

"But you're walking so fast, Clarise . . . But hey! You're Guyanese — you *always* walk slowly, Mavis walks slowly . . . You're running away! Wait one cotton-pickin' minute! You understand, you know and you don't want to discuss it. Well, Clarise, I'm too old to keep up with you. I've become like the Guyanese, I've learned to walk slowly, take it cool. To breeze! *Free-up myself!* Is that what you say?

"Look! Please, Clarise, please. I know you're not in this much of a hurry. Come with me, here's a cafeteria. Let's have a cup of coffee, come . . ."

Clarise feel Mr. Blades take her arm and she feel

herself going with him and like she don't have any power in her two feet to stop herself from walking and going with him. She want to say *No! Wait! Stop right here!* and put down her two feet, like pon this round thing in the pavement here, right here, and say:

"Wait! Mr. Blades?"

"What? Come, please, Clarise, let's sit and chat. I promise, I'll tell you anything you want to know. Look at me, would I lie to you? Here's the place, let's go inside."

Clarise look at Mr. Blades and he smile. She look for the guilt. She don't see it. Is de guilt-in-de-face, in de eyes, that does always make you know de sly-ones from de all-right-ones, she say in her mind. But he all right, she tell herself, and she walk with him inside to a table. He say:

"Come, you can choose your own cake."

"Pone? Any pone?"

"What's that?"

"Cassava-pone."

"Cassa *what*? Oh, that's delightful! Ha-ha-ha! Ho-ho-ho!"

Eh-eh! Well, like he properly get *tickle*. Is what tickling he so? All I say was . . . ohhh, yes! They mustbe don't have ground-provisions here? Ow Lawd! There you go again, Clarise chile. Po'-country-come-to-town. Talking stupidness. But . . . ain't I see cassava in Brooklyn? Still . . .

"I shame!"

"For what? You must *never* be ashamed, Clarise, never with me."

And Mr. Blades put his arm round Clarise shoulder and he draw her to him and he squeeze. It feel nice and comfortable.

They get the cake and the coffee and a very ole lady with a saucer of cake in her hand tottering up to her chair smile at Clarise and Clarise smile back and pull out her chair for her.

When they sit down at the table facing one-another, Mr. Blades say:

"Now, do you want to ask me or tell?" And he take something in a lil bottle from his pocket and put it in his coffee.

"What is that?" Clarise ask.

"What? Oh, this? Saccharin. I've been using it as a sugar substitute for years; now they tell me it causes cancer. Well, to hell with it, I say. If you take the word of the FDA —"

"What is FDA?"

"The Food and Drug Administration. They regulate . . . But wait, not now, please, later for that. Right now I want you to tell me about yourself, Clarise, and before we clear the air of everything else, let me relieve my mind of this: I'm extremely attracted to you."

"Why?"

"Why? Why? You're a beautiful woman, and what's more I think you know it. You know, don't you?"

"But that is not what we come here to talk —"

"You led me, you asked me a question."

"Okay, but is you first ask. I answering. Yes, I want to ask questions but not bout you and me. They ain't got nothing like you and me. Is you and Mavis, and me and Mavis, and is so you and me get to be sitting down here today. So lehwe talk bout why you can't tell Mavis. Is what you meaning when you say it would spoil our friendship?"

"To answer that I'll have to tell you about my relationship with Mavis."

Then Mr. Blades start to talk and Clarise watch his face. He is a sweet ole man, she say to herself. Mavis too damn *dotish* with sheself like she never hear what de ole people say: *"Better be a ole man sweetheart than a young man slave."* All she want is money and gratification . . .

Eh-eh! But watch me using de man big-words.

He talking. He look like something out of a picture. Look at his lil beard and his black-and-white hair and watch de two eyes how they burning when he talking. He resemble Mr. Hudson without de curly hair . . . Is so I use to watch Mr. Hudson face when he talking to me . . . Harold? Is where you, dear? Is where, is where is where you is in de whole-wide-world, Harold? You running from me? Stop running . . . Stop! Wait! Lehwe talk. It ain't so bad as all that. We could work it out . . .

"You're not listening to me at all, you're thinking about your husband, right?"

"Yes!"

"Any chance of finding him?"

"It don't look so sometimes. I getting tired."

"Look! The last Saturday night next month there's a party at the Tilden Ballroom. We can go, the three of us, you, Mavis, and me. She's always complaining that I don't take her out dancing, but at my age I can have my music at home . . ."

I know how you like to dance, Clarise say in her mind, and she smile at what Mavis say to her bout him. Ow! Poor man.

"We'll go, and perhaps you'll get some word there about Harold. Okay?"

"A party? No. But any news bout Harold will be welcome."

"And the money?"

"Not unless Mavis know."

"But you agree with me now that she's —"

"No, I don't agree and I will find a way to tell her that you offer me —"

"Well, why can't you tell her straight out?"

"Cause she is a *touchous* lady!"

"See?"

"She is my friend, sir!"

"Yes, that's the difference, you see, Clarise. She is not *my* friend and I was not lying to you when I told you I tried. I've been trying from the first day I met her to be a friend to her. But I know what it is . . ."

"What it is?"

"It's that group of women she cohorts with every weekend."

"Ohhh! You mean where de women does go and talk? Yes . . . I wish I had de time."

"Christ! These women chew up men and spit 'em out!"

"How you know, Mr. Blades? You ever been to a meeting, I mean? I thought they say men don't go."

"We daren't!"

"I *sure* that is not true. Why y'all don't go and see before you talk? You *know* how much thing you could settle so?"

"Settle what? What can you settle with a woman who thinks it's funny to mail her husband's dirty drawers to his girlfriend?"

"His drawers, Mr. Blades? But men don't wear —"

"His underpants."

"You call it . . . ?"

"Yes we do, here . . . So this man — now, I'm telling it as Mavis reports it being told at her previous group meeting — the man must've had some kind of argu-

141

ment with his wife over the girlfriend. The wife claims he told her that his girlfriend is younger, smarter, and prettier than her, and apart from that, she doesn't nag him. And what's more, she loves his *dirty drawers.* So do you know what that bitch *did?*"

"Bitch? Which bitch?"

"The man's wife. She took a pair of her husband's dirty drawers and mailed it to that other woman because, as Mavis told me with great hilarity — and I'm quoting Mavis now, who was quoting the wife who spoke at the women's meeting — the husband's dirty drawers have 'the bouquet of a latrine and the texture of a burlap bag.'

" 'See if you still love him now,' was the message she put in the package. Now *you* tell me: what can *any* man settle with a woman like that? Damn! They're downright *frightening!* But Mavis, *my* woman, relates this with great hilarity. She thinks it very funny, and just."

"But I think it funny too. You *self,* Mr. Blades, that is not a funny story?"

"Of course, it may be funny to you women, but I keep seeing myself in the man's place, you see? Especially with Mavis to deal with."

"You marry, Mr. Blades?"

"Yes, I am."

"And what your wife does say bout Mavis?"

"I managed to keep them apart. But stories like that one scare the hell out of me. Let me tell you another one that came out of those meetings:

"This woman got pregnant by a man who's playing the fool with her. She aborts the child, puts the fetus in a shoe box, goes to his house, rings the doorbell, puts the shoe box in his wife's hands, and says, 'This belongs to your husband. Please give it to him for me.'

"She's not down the path yet when she hears that poor woman screaming. But she has planned it so she's leaving town, has all her things packed in her car. She splits, leaving the man in a hell of a mess, yes, but what about the poor wife? *Isn't she a woman too?* Where's the sisterly love? That's what I want to know, where's the sisterly love?"

"Ohhh! Ow, Mr. Blades, Mavis won't *ever* do a thing like . . ."

"No? No, no, she won't, Clarise . . . Now! What are *you* going to do? It's too late to go for an interview at any agency now, and you didn't really miss an appointment earlier, did you?"

"No, sir. Is so sometimes I would just walk and walk and walk forgetting what I have to do. Sometimes I find m'self in de street just staring at all de things . . . I never see so much things in my *whole life!* No! F'truth, Mr. Blades . . ."

"Look, Clarise, this 'Mr. Blades' is getting to me. Curleigh, call me Curleigh."

"Okay, Mr. Blades . . . If only you coulda see Guyana? You would know what I mean when I say it have things like *bush* in this America. Y'know when you go in de bush and all y'could see is jungle-bush? Is so here stay. But down there some parts does have a lil river and some waterfalls and rocks-in-between and you does hear de birds singing . . . Blades? I mean Curleigh? . . ."

Mr. Blades throw back his head and laugh and Clarise wonder if he laughing at what she saying or how she call his name wrong.

"So, you go wandering through all this jungle of New York searching for your little rivulets and waterfalls . . . And tell me, dear, sweet Clarise . . . I could fall in love with you so easily, do you know that?"

"If I know what, Mr. Blades?"

"You heard me . . ."

"Yes, sir, but I wasn't sure."

"And what will you say — now that you're sure, I mean? Now you've heard me say that I'll do anything in the world for you. You just have to call on me. Anytime, Clarise. I'm your friend. What do you have to say to that?"

"That sometimes, some times, I does find the lil peace I looking for here. Sometimes, simple so . . . Like today I see you and I talk. Just a nice talk. I don't agree with all you have to say. I don't like how you like to call women *bitch* all de time, cause if woman is bitch, you is a son-of-a-bitch. I play like I not hearing when you bringing up anything to confuse my mind. But just seeing you so and talking is nice and relaxing.

"Y'know what? A day, a nice day, like today? Was de first of May. May Day at home, with de parades and so . . . It was de first day I really notice how New York could be nice, cause I just decide to forget myself and sit in de park and stare. Forget my cares. Forget all de sorrying-for-m'self cause I can't find a decent job and so.

"I mustbe was talking to myself hard, cause a lady sitting next to me suddenly break through my thoughts. She tell me she come from a place name *Afghanistan*. You know there?"

"Of course! It's horrible what's going on there."

"She say she is refugee and that de Russians drive her out her country since nineteen seventy-eight and that it could happen to me. Mr. Blades? That lady tell me so much *horrors* bout what happening in her country, I stop feeling so sorry for m'self that day. All I say is I want to go home and help make sure it don't happen to we. Is funny how hearing other people troubles that worse than yours could make you feel better . . .

"And like today? Sitting here talking to you? Just seeing you so and talking? Relax me nice . . .

"And sometimes? — not only that day with de woman from Afghanistan — I would sit down in de park, any park I come to, and just look at de people passing. New York full of crazypeople, eh? Eh-eh! I thought was only in Guyana people going out they head every day. Look, Mr. Curleigh? You should *see* some of these people! You just left them good good, sane-as-ever, say, sometime last week. Next-thing-you-know? You going butt-up with them and is clean *out!* They gone outa they mind. As Miz Barr de schoolmistress does say: *'Another-one bite de dust!'*

"Well, sitting down in de park here in New York y'could see them too. We have one in Guyana, they call him de Politician: 'In nineteen fifty-three, Jagan seh . . . In nineteen sixty-three, Burnham seh . . . In nineteen seventy-three, Jagan and Burnham *did* seh . . . This is nineteen eighty-three and *me* seh . . .' And he holding his hand like a microphone and telling you all what de politicians 'seh' and if you listen him good, he making sense."

"What kind of sense? What's he saying?"

"What he saying? He saying is *all* lies. One-set-of-*lies* cause nothing don't make sense when you add-it-all-up. Everything everybody saying is lies. But you have to listen him good or else he talking stupidness, he mad.

"I don't know America story, but is de same thing one of allyuh own here been saying in that park near Twenty-third Street de other day. He was bad-talking that president allyuh had here. Y'know? De one that did break-and-enter de water gate. We hear bout it *still* in Guyana."

"He did *what*? Ha!" Mr. Blades laugh and say, "Clarise, you're precious."

"He did dress-up like he mad and he talking all over he face but I had de time so I sit and listen and I hear him talk de lies y'all does hear from them here, too. Is why they does have to fool de people, Curleigh?"

"Because if they told the truth they would not be able to govern, Clarise. The truth in politics is not for the people's ear. Sometimes they're better off not knowing the truth. But tell me about —"

"I does go right there in de park to sit down and say my prayers, to ask all de powers that guiding me through this life here to help me get a job. I just had a interview with de man, Mr. Jacobson, to get a cleaning-job at de antiquestore nearby here, and he tell me was to check with him . . . Friday! Ohhh God! Is today, is today! I did *feel* I had something important to do. Is how I could forget a thing like that?"

"I'm to blame. I swept you off your feet, didn't I? Good! I'm happy. But I don't want you to miss out on a job because . . . This man, Mr. What's-his —"

"Jacobson."

"For what?"

"To find out if he has de cleaning-job for me, if I get de work, if he giving it to me."

"Ohhh . . . He was still interviewing, perhaps. What's the address?" Mr. Blades look at Clarise paper. "Oh, but that's just a block away . . . Wait a minute, where were you coming from when I saw you?"

"Two hundred and seventeen Broadway. I had another ap —"

"Where? Walking?"

"Yes."

"Since when? This morning? Hell! Come, my love. Walk with me one more block and go see that man. You look radiant, with beads of sweat like pearls on your lip, there . . ."

Mr. Blades take his kerchief and touch it to Clarise top lip while he saying:

"Go, woman, and tell him how much you need that job to find your man. He'll give it to you. And I'll see you at the dance? . . . Remember, keep the date free. Louise Bennett will be performing. Do you know her?"

"No, I don't know her, but I like to hear her and Paul Keynes Douglas and Habeeb Khan and . . . it does be real *ganga-time* when they start-up."

"Good! She'll be on that night. She's the only reason I'm bending to Mavis — and your problem, of course. We'll all go."

"But Curleigh . . . I don't feel like going no dance. My mind too —"

"It will clear it. You're going there for a reason, too. Remember? Someone there *must* know. We'll have it announced onstage. Something will turn up . . . You should come along. You won't regret it. Here's my telephone number and address on this card. You call me and tell me when you've got that job. And I'll see you at the dance.

"And remember, Clarise, any thing, any time. You only have to ask. Remember that . . ."

When Clarise daughter Eunice was a lil girl she use to say, "Mammie, I feel like a yum!"

She get that from her father. She grow up saying it cause she always hearing it. And when Harold feel like that? He ain't got no business what the money set aside for — *he have to have he rum!* He just *have* to have it. Clarise use to try to explain to him that you can't put rum in the pot.

But what? He just had to have his rum.

Well, is so I feeling tonight, Clarise say to herself. I have to have a *yum.* I have to celebrate this. Is de beginning-of-de-end, and I celebrating . . .

She ask for Guyana-rum at the liquorstore. But the man say he is a lover-of-rum but he never hear bout no brandname like King-o-Diamond, XM, or El-Dorado. Clarise tell him if he is a lover-of-rum and he ain't taste XM Ten-Year-Old or El-Dorado Bonded Reserve, she feel sorry for him, but she promise whenever she see a bottle to bring him a taste.

The man laugh and say, "That's a promise now, you hear?" and he give her a bottle of Bacardi.

Is Clarise hustling home rejoicing cause she find a job and remembering what Mr. Jacobson say:

"I'm glad you came, Miss Cumberbatch, I was waiting for your call."

"Sir?"

"You have the job."

"Thank you. Where you want me to start?" Clarise say as calm as ever. This time if you did *hear* her heart going buddupbuddupbup!

"Ha-ha!" Mr. Jacobson laugh. "No, please come on Monday at nine," he say.

"Mavis, I find a job I find a job I find a job! I find *work!* Mavis! Come and lehwe have a *chups!*"

Is Clarise bursting through the door, holding up the Bacardi and shouting for joy . . .

"Now I can pay you back your money, buy new

panty, send home a barrel, and save up my passage to go home . . . Oh! I see Curleigh today, y'know?"

"Yes, is so he say. But Clarise, I had a *hard* day and I ain't feel to drink or talk."

"All right, Mavis. But tonight is a special night. You will take just *one* to celebrate, right?"

"Okay, but only one."

Clarise make some lemonade and mix two drinks. She give Mavis one and say:

"Wait! First lemme ring Curleigh and tell he."

When she get off the phone, Mavis say:

"Hmmm, de two-you *proper cozy* . . ."

Twelve

Look! I tired of these deady deady Friday night stick-up-in-de-house watching "Muppet Show" and talking de same-ole-story . . . Is *party* it want round here, hear? Is a *party* it need tonight . . . Lehwe nice-up de place . . . Lemme wine-up me waist . . .

"Y'hear me?"

"You hear me?"

CLICK!

Is Mavis turn-off the TV put-on her stereo-music.

> BAM!
> Bam!
> Dis-a-session-o-de
> RAM!
> Everyone's gonna jam
> JAM!

a-dis-ya-session-o-de-ram
RAM!
Every
WOMAN!
every
MAN!
gonna-rock-it-in-a-bam
BAM! . . .
Ya-hear-me?
Ya-hear-me?
COME!
Just-come-and-lehwe-jam
JAM!
a-dis-ya-session-o . . .

Is Mavis pounce pon her telephone and calling up her friends:

"Is you, Edris? And where Stars-and-Stripes? All-yuh home? Must-come man, allyuh must come . . . Is a party. Nutting special. Just to cheer up my friend Clarise, and so allyuh could meet she. So long she here . . .

"Eh-eh! Yes, is tonight, not tomorrow night. Cause tomorrow I got to do de washing and de shopping and go to my meeting . . . No . . . Is tonight. Tonight is it. Must come! Bring a bottle of whatever y'drinking. Come nine, ten o'clock . . . And listen! I ain't cooking, so eat first!"

Is one after the other Mavis calling up her friends:

"Polish? Is you? You *still* here? Well, come and lehwe jam, boy! You too damn *common* with y'self . . . I ain't looking after no man, I don't want no man. All I want is to *enjoy* m'self . . . Polish, good God! Suppose I was to tell your wife all these things you telling me?

But too-besides all these years she mustbe know already that you is a *manwhore!* Ha! But must come, man, must come! Yes . . ."

"Is same time like last time and remember to . . ."

"Eat first! Cause I know how you long-belly and I ain't into no cooking tonight. All I looking after is de sport . . ."

". . . nutting, n'occasion! Is only my friend from Guyana . . . She depress . . . Is to cheer her up! No, she don't want no man to do it. Just keep he that-side by you . . . Who? But is since when your hands does *too* full?" Mavis screaming pon the phone.

". . . Debbie, is either you getting ole or you forgetting your ole tricks . . . Or take care you into something else? . . ."

". . . Well, if he want a woman to jam, tell he this one don't want no man. She got a husband already . . . Yes, chile, de same time like de last time . . . *eat first* . . ."

". . . What is that you say, Bibi? Permanent-secretary visiting from home? Well, let him visit somewhere else. I don't want no *government-people* at my party. No politics not talking in my drawingroom. *That thing does break-up sport.* Cause is everybody who in America running-de-government from here does have to put in they three-cents. Last time? When de arguments and de cussing-out and screaming-down start? Is my nice nice tablefoot get break-up. No! Guyana-story like *duck-story:* it ain't got no ending. So keep your permanent-secretary . . ."

"Clarise, man, put on some nice calypso or a reggae or something. It have a Mary Isaacs there — play that: 'A Little of Heaven'! Play something going make me feel nice. I strickly into *bubbling* tonight . . . We all going bubble, right?"

Clarise playing music:

> When ah drinking me rum
> don't talk to me . . .

and she listening conversation cause like nobody don't want to dance. Like is everybody have something they have to get off they mind.

Is Polish: "I talking bout de sun going down in de west like a bar of gold over de mountains. And over that? — y'all not going believe this, y'all going say is de same ole story — a *dark* cloud like a line-drawing in de sky . . . a *pork-knocker,* with a *warishi* pon he back, boy!"

"Polish, Polish, Polish! *Jeez-us-Christ!* Polish, give we a break now, man. Is how come you see so much golden-nugget and sunset and you still here catching-ass with de rest o' we? *You* was that pork-knocker with de warishi-basket pon he back, Polish. Is how come you come here and y'stay?" Stars-and-Stripes asking.

"Hmmmmm!" Polish throw up his hands then bring them down hard pon his knees. " 'Where there is no vision, de people perish,' " he say. Then he turn round looking for help. He and Clarise eye make four.

"Sister," Polish say, "you ever been in de bush?"

Clarise nod her head up and down.

"Well tell these . . . these . . . *townpeople* . . . these *coast-dwellers* . . . tell them I ain't lying. Please . . ."

Clarise continue to nod her head but she don't say nothing. But everybody in the room could see that she agree with all Polish saying.

Polish turn back to the rest and say:

"See? She know, she been. Y'all don't know nothing. Jeez-us! Is true what de man say: 'Where there is no vision, de people perish!' But forgive them, Lord, they only ignorant."

Them ain't *only* ignorant, Clarise say in her mind. Them feel they have too much in this country to give up and can't see nobody wanting to do that just to go back home. And to de *bush*, too-*besides*? Praise Christ I ain't got no long long motorcar and nuff . . . Eh-eh! But wait! Is now I remember this thing . . . now I come to this country and find out how thing could get *falsify* here . . . I wonder if that motorcar Harold and Leonie was posing in front in de snapshot that they send home to show-off with was really they own? Or mustbe was borrow they did borrow it?

Ow Lawd! Look how life does turn, eh? Is such a *long* time since I did see de first one them pictures. Now look me here listening tonight and wondering how I could get back where I come from. Look! If I was de woman I is now and not who I was then? I woulda just throw de damn pictures oneside and keep on stepping with my life . . . like I intends to do now . . .

Is talk Clarise talking to herself till she hear somebody bawling:

"Ow, Polish, enough is enough! Ease-up lil bit now, man."

And somebody else bawling:

"De man like you, Stripes. Polish just like you. He is a *Post-Independence-Casualty-Case* like you. Like you forget how you get your name? 'On de twenty-six of May nineteen sixty-six, when de Golden Arrowhead unfoil, my heart start to boil. But y'see when that arrowhead start to jook me? And it jook me it jook me it jook me . . . till all I could see was *Stars-and-Stripes!*' "

"Do it again, Bugs! Do it again!" Everybody begging Bugs and laughing at his antics. And somebody ask:

"Is who did say that?"

"Andre Soobryan, boy. De best stand-up comedian in Guyana and de whole-wide-world," Bugs say.

And Polish like he get vex, cause he burst out sudden:

"I'm not any Post-Independence-Casualty-Case! I came to this country to get a education."

"Ain't y'get it? So is what y'still doing here? Is what you still here for?" Edris say. "Is why y'all men does *fool* y'self so, eh? You like *me*, Polish, you *like* it here! That's why you stay. Is *like* you like it here."

"Naaaa, man! De man ain't like it here. He like *me*. Is left he get left here," Jacko say. "He like me. He mustbe ain't even got de passage money and is left he —"

"Y'*lie!* Jacko, you lie like a ASS! Is fraid you fraid to test de bogus passport you buy."

"And *you* use your bogus greencard, Mavis? Is who tell you you got more balls than me?"

Is Mavis party in full swing. And Clarise now sitting down in a corner near to Curleigh listening, and somebody saying:

". . . that is what they does do, give you de money with one hand and de terms in de other."

"Yeah!" Polish say. "And they ask you to devalue your already valueless dollar and cut down on de labor-force in some of your most labor-intensive industries. And what they doing there is socking-it-to-de-poor! That is what that all bout. And next thing you know? De people turning on de government . . ."

"That ain't aid, man, that is fuck-up!" somebody shout out from the toilet same time he flush it.

"Yeah, why you think people starting to call them de International MF?" Polish say.

"Yeah, de Stars-and-Stripes and de Golden-Arrow-head," Bugs say.

Is Mavis in the kitchen getting ice and fretting:

"Y'see? Y'see? Is talk they talking de *politics,* in my house, Lawd! I *beg* them. I *beseech* them . . . But y'hearing them? And when I throw they ass out de house? Everybody going say I bad, Mavis bad . . ."

"Don't feel no way, Mavis. Is *all* politics. You can't get away from it, sister. Look at de suffering of de brothers and sisters in South Africa? Look at de international piracy and terrorism. Look at de *plunder* of de resources of de people of Africa, of Guyana, Jamaica? De natural gift of *Ja!*

"Is politics, Mavis. But don't dig! After all is said-and-done, Rasta is King! Lord of Lord, Conquering Lion of de Tribe of Judah, a'ya! I-man *Overs* Babylon . . ."

"Ohhh, Jesus! Help me!" Mavis say.

"Jesus ain't going help you . . . Ja-Ja, Mavis! I-and-I are *Conqueror* . . ."

"Steewpps!" Mavis suck her teeth. Mavis walk out in the middle of the people stuff-up in her drawing-room, she plunk the icebucket down on the lil bar in the corner, and she say:

"Clarise, you playing de music here? Put on a Sparrow calypso, please."

Clarise say in her mind, Ow, Mavis, is why you don't let de people talk? You and me both might learn something. But anyway, she put on the music. And when Sparrow start up with ". . . capitalism gone mad!":

"No, not *that,* please, Clarise!" Mavis scream. "That is *more* thing for them to make talk pon . . ."

But nobody not taking Mavis on. Polish saying:

"De whole damn world like it falling apart as far's

156

I'm concerned. Guyana is de only place with a center, f'me, at least. These blasted superpowers with they bag of dirty-expansionist-meddling tricks . . . Every oppressed person ought to rise up against this shit! Every *Yid!* Every dumb Polack, according to Archie Bunker, every *nigger, faggot . . .*"

Polish stop talking, then:

"Look!" he say. "I had a experience in this city. Listen, hear how these people operating: A man come to me once and tell me he have nine million dollars to buy G's —"

"To buy what?" Mavis say, cause she listening now.

"G's, Mavis, G's," Jacko say. "Guyana currency, Mavis. You doanno *nutting?*"

"Look, you —" Mavis beginning to cuss, but,

"Listen!" Polish say. "Listen to this good. It going show you how these people does operate . . . He say he have nine million dollars to buy —"

"In U.S., Polish? Is U.S.? Nine million U.S.?"

"*Uncle Sam*'s, son. Y'damn right, y'know is immediately I start to multiply by ten, at *least* ten. Cause I say this kinda deal is not no bank-to-bank deal unless he have good reasons that I can't even speculate pon, and he ain't offering to share with me . . . So I tell de man, I say: 'Here, fella, you know Guyana money is *Monopoly* money? It can't buy nothing nowhere but there, y'know?' "

"And what he say?"

Everybody asking Polish that question because they all listening now.

"Now I have to tell you, this man my friend, right? I mean, he *befriend* me, and he do me a lot of kindness . . . Ahhh, boy, I wish I had a witness to this. But de only witness I have dead. He —"

"Shit, man! Talk your story, nuh? Is why y'all Guyanese like dig-up dead so? Let de dead rest easy."

Is Jacko say so.

"Okay," Polish say. "So when I tell de man is Monopoly money, and he tell me he still want it, I ask he is f'what? Destabilization? Or to buy Guyana prawns-catch from midocean before it could reach de shore? Or what?

"Look! Hey-ya! Boy, lehwe forget this story, hear? This story got *too much melody,*" Polish say.

"Yes! *Forget* it in my house! You, Polish, always starting-up story. Well, I ain't got no tablefoot to break-up . . . Is time y'all go home . . . EVERYBODY OUT!"

"Mavis, sit down and shut up, let de man finish he story, nuh! Boy Polish boy go on, we listening. Mavis *kankawa!*"

"Ohhh, is me? Is me who kankawa! Is me who come to America and study

"metallurgy

"and geology

"and miner-

"ology . . . and all-them-other-ologies! And is me who going back to Guyana to go stick-me-head in de bush? . . ."

"Hey, Polish, Mavis does talk stupidness, but she got a point there," Bugs say. "Is why you going back there? What you going do, man —"

"HOLD DE FUCKING FORT, FOOL!" Polish scream. "I telling allyuh *this shit like it hitting de fan!* But allyuh ain't listening . . . When de people ain't got nowhere else to go, they going come again. Remember Jonestown?"

"Polish . . ." Edris say.

"Yes?"

"You did tell anybody bout de money? De nine million U.S. for de G's?"

"Yes . . ."

"Is who you —"

"Edris, that subject is *closed,* hear?"

"Hey, Polish, y'know what?"

"What, Jacko?"

"Your friend . . ."

"Which one?"

"De one who was trying to fuck-up de country . . ."

"Yeah?"

"He mustbe one them International MF's, eh?"

"International MF or CIA, you mean . . . But too-besides, *is all de same.*"

"Polish, get your ass out my house now. Now now, please. Just now Bibi going come with *she* cross, and my drawingroom going —"

"To hell with you and your drawingroom, Mavis," Jacko say. "Polish boy, talk if you talking . . ."

"Eh-eh! But *hear* this man! Like is *he* paying de rent here. Is you paying my rent, Jacko?"

"Shit, is not *me* make I ain't paying it. I *ask* you several times, but you say you don't want no bad-fash-ion Guyanese man no more. Is cause y'can't get *control* of us, right, Mavis? And you have to have contr —"

"Shut-up-and-get-your-ass-out-my-house   NOW, Jacko! Now! Here, take your coat . . . No, I not laugh-ing . . . No . . . *don't touch me!*"

Is Mavis cussing Jacko and pushing him to the door. Everybody see she serious and they get up to go but nobody don't want to go. You could see it in the way they calling out to one-another still:

"Boy, what you think bout that Grenada-thing?"

". . . When last you been to Georgetown? I ain't getting no news from GT these days. Y'did hear bout . . ."

You could see that these people glad to sit and talk

159

bout home, even them who saying they not going back, *glad* to hear the talk . . . But Mavis chucking them out the house, and everybody could see is Jacko she vex with more than anybody else.

Is break Mavis party breaking-up so, before it even start good yet, and Curleigh in the corner near Clarise saying:

"Oh, Clarise, I think it was Kipling who said, 'We meet in an evil land, close to the gates of hell.' It's a pity . . . If only we could meet again, somewhere else . . . You haven't said a word tonight. Why?"

"I didn't have nothing to say."

"I *bet* you did, Clarise, I bet you did."

And Curleigh take Clarise hand into both of his own in the confusion of the talk and the doorbell ringing and Mavis telling Bibi and the permanent-secretary:

"Allyuh too late! Allyuh could go to Larry's Liquid Love round de corner and free-up y'self and talk all de politics y'all want to talk. This here ain't no club."

"Ow, Mavis," Polish say. "I coulda ask de man some questions bout de Gold-Board! I —"

"Go Larry's," Mavis say. "Allyuh go . . ."

"But I want to find out bout re-migration benefits. If —"

"Go!" Mavis say. "And *you too,* Curleigh Blades. That is, if you done making love to Clarise."

"If only we could meet somewhere else, Clarise," Curleigh say, when Mavis turn back to make sure everybody believe she mean what she saying. "In Guyana, perhaps?" Curleigh say.

"Not where I going," Clarise say.

"And where is that?"

"In de bush."

"It sounds *wonderful* to me. I'd go *any* place with you, Clarise."

160

"You only think so, Curleigh . . . But look! Everybody gone and Mavis waiting . . ."

Curleigh lift Clarise hand to his face and kiss her in the palm. Then he look at Mavis standing with her hand pon her hip waiting with the door open and the other hand pon the doorknob, saying:

"Yes, you too, Mr. Blades. I tired."

"Okay! Okay, okay, okay, boss!" Curleigh say to Mavis. "I wish you could have let it go a little longer, though. I was enjoying it . . . A global socioeconomic view of our condition, Mavis. I'm American, not Guyanese, but what these people were saying also affects my condition as a black man in —"

"Ohhh . . ."

"Okay, Mavis, I'm going. I'm going right now. *Goodbye*, Mavis!" Curleigh say and then he turn back to Clarise.

"Remember, anything, I'll be there, okay?"

Mavis say she don't want to talk, so Clarise help her to clean-up the place in silence. Only she thinking thinking thinking.

The next day Clarise wake up she *still* thinking thinking. And she go to the bathroom and she look her face in the mirror and she say:

"Dear God, save my country for me. Save de bush, save my children, save de world. I ain't even *start to live yet*, Lawd! Save my home for me. Save all o' we," cause like she can't get something out her mind . . .

Was a morning, and she was leaving the house to go to the market to buy some fish to cook Harold breakfast. She was just walking out the backdoor, "One Day at a Time" just done play when the radio say:

"We will now go to Radio Free Grenada for a report . . ." Then:

"Fellow Grenadians, we must not let this happen. The Americans are here! They have invaded our sovereign nation. They are here on our soil. You must come out and stop them!

"We must not let this happen to us, fellow Grenadians. You doctors, nurses, citizens who love your country, come out and help stop them . . ."

Was a woman.

Was a man.

Was two people screaming, crying, pon the radio. Then:

Click!

They gone off the air. They get cut off. Was what?

Clarise hear people saying this-and-that. Some say the Grenadians was glad to see the Americans come. Some say that the fighting go on all up-in-the-hills and the Grenadians tearing them American tail. Clarise don't know *who* to believe.

When she come here, Mavis say that she see it pon the TV and the Grenadians was *glad* and welcoming the American troops. But is not Mavis-self say to her that she mustn't believe all she see pon the TV?

Ow Lawd! All I know, Lawd, is what I know. And I never been to highschool, so I don't know much, Clarise say to herself. All I know is what I hear: them two people pon de radio begging de people to come out and try to stop de invasion, begging for help, begging for . . .

MERCY! Lawd.

STOP!

ENOUGH!

PLEASE!

All I remember is that woman from Af-ghan-is-tan, that day in de park talking to me. I remember what she say . . .

162

Lawd! Save we country f'we, please . . . ?

And day after day after day, month after month after month, Clarise waking up every morning praying justso in front her mirror. Is over a year gone now since she come to America. She see Christmas, and not one drop of snow ain't fall like pon de Christmas cards. Not till long after Christmas they get snow. She send home a barrel and say she saving to come home. She working working working, but like she not seeing her way to get up the passage-money and all the things she need to take back with her too.

She want to talk it over with Mavis but she not sure how Mavis going take it. But Clarise is not the one to take-she-stomach-make-bankhouse, so one night she say:

"Mavis? You sleeping?"

"Jeezus, Mary, and Joseph!" Mavis groan.

"Mavis, I going home . . ."

"YOU GOING WHERE?"

Is Mavis fly out her sleep, out her bed, screaming so, cause Clarise say she going home.

"Yes, Mavis. Home, home to Guyana, Mavis. Look, just go and look under de bed, see what you going see . . . Why you think I insisting pon sweeping de house every Saturday now? Is so you won't have to look under de bed . . . Eunice letter convince me. Is no use I using up my substance in this country looking for Harold Cumberbatch. And after your party? While I looking for a better job? I was shopping, too — you didn't know that. Look! Look under de bed, Mavis . . ."

"What is this?"

BRAM!

"What is this, and . . ."

PLANG!

163

". . . this . . . and that?"

BRANG-PLANG!

"That? . . . Is what?"

Is a rake.

Is a shovel!

Is a prospecting-knife and a batelle.

Is a file.

Eh-eh!

"What is this?"

Is Mavis pon her belly pulling them from under the bed and tossing them out, screaming:

"Is what-de-hell is all this?"

"Is gold, Mavis! These is de things you need to work gold. Next week? When I get pay? I going buy a suru-kha-sieve. Is gold, Mavis, it better than de American dollar."

"What better than . . . WHAT STUPIDNESS YOU TALKING, CLARISE? I can't stand it! I can't stand it I can't STAND IT!"

Eh-eh!

Is Mavis pelting everything pon her dressing-case at Clarise.

Is a bottle of Joy.

Is a powderbowl and it powderpuff.

Is a hairbrush and a pincushion.

Is a —

"No, Mavis!"

Is Clarise shout-out quick! And Mavis stop, look at the thing in her hand . . .

Is a curling iron.

Ow!

"Ow, Clarise, I coulda *kill* you!"

"You see now, Mavis? But what happen, Mavis," Clarise ask. "What happen? All I say is that I going home. Is what I do you?"

"You want to hear, Clarise? You really *want* to hear?"

"I *must* want to hear, Mavis, you is my friend. The best friend I ever had, but is what I do to you to hurt you so? Tell me . . . talk all! Please? I want to hear."

"Don't worry, man, let it pass. Lehwe forget this story, hear?"

Mavis turn away and bend down. She start picking up the things on the floor. Clarise catch her by her shoulder.

"No, Mavis! Come, talk now, we can't live so. What happen? Is what I do? How we could just forget tonight? Justso? No! Tell me, Mavis, tell me. If is anything I can explain? Let me help you . . . Cause I don't want to cause you no strain.

"Is cause I staying here? Is that, or what? Is cause I can only get cleaning-job? But I still pay you back all your money, right? So why? Ow, man, don't shy with me . . . Is me. Is Clarise, your friend. Is me . . . De two o' we, remember? You and me how we use to —"

"Ohhh, Clarise, Clarise, Clarise, ahhhhh!"

Is Mavis bust-out cry!

"Oh my! Mavis? Mavis? Is what is what is what? Tell me!" Clarise say, and Mavis start to talk:

"You coming to America . . . When I hear? I glad bad, cause I say Clarise coming, my friend, my love, Clarise, coming. I say I don't know why she only coming to search for that man, but she coming and that is enough for me. Clarise, I talk bout you till my woman get jealous. Yes, my *woman*, Clarise. Bella is my woman and she jealous you. But I don't care, cause I love you, Clarise. I love you more than any woman, any woman I *ever* love. I love you when I vex with you, I love you when I quarreling with you, I love you when I sucking-up my teeth pon you, when you talking and doing all your foolishness — which is y'know is your thing! — I love you. But all I ever hear you talk bout is Harold Harold Harold Harold.

"I hear Harold Cumberbatch name till I want to choke pon it, but I *bear my chafe*. I cuss-and-bear-it. Cuss and bear. My man, Mr. Blades, stop coming. He use to come *every night* and I know till you come he was just crazy over me. Now you come he can't wait to get in your drawers. He don't give me no money no more. I say he giving you . . . If I didn't know how you stay? I'da say is you getting it from he instead of me. But I know you won't do that. And now? When I just settling down to my life with you now, when I get accustom to you? Now when I . . .

"Ohhh God! Clarise, don't go? Please don't go? Don't go don't go don't go don't go ohhh! Don't go, please."

"Mavis Mavis Mavis Mavis Mavis! Humhmhmhmhm. My love my love my love, my sweet sweet sweet Mavis, Mavis Mavis Mavis. I sorry! I am sooo sorry, m'sister, ohhh-ohhh-ow! Mavis, Mavis Mavis. Ow ow ow ow! Ow, Mavis! I *really* sorry, chile . . ."

And is so Clarise pon the floor with her sister, her friend Mavis, rocking her in her arms and cooing to her like she talking to a baby . . .

Ow Lawd! Is why this life have to be so complicate? Is how I going live with Mavis now? Is how me going undress in front of she and she going be in de same room with me without somebody, some one o' we feeling uncomfortable or holding something back?

Ow Lawd!

Is a pity. Cause was so nice at Mavis. So nice and comfortable like home. And not expensive . . . Look how much for rent in New York now! And you can't even get . . . *That* is it, too! You can't get house to rent in New York and when you do? Is who is you to be paying three-four-five-hundred-dollars-a-month in some chokey-hole full of roach and rat and every day you hearing pon de radio, seeing pon de TV, how the ass-best-us killing people in de city? And you watching it peel off de heatpipe before your eye . . .

Hummm hummm hummm!

. . . And in that, de same apartment building? People paying through they teeth to live with roach and rat and get they dead! Forget that! I going home. To ass with Harold Cumberbatch! If he come back, I will take he back . . . but I ain't looking fo' he *no more!*

No!

Look at all them wild-goose-chase he lead me pon. Look at all them mechanic shop and gas stations office building and stone quarry I had to . . .

Sorry, Harry! I ain't no fool. Something wrong! Is every place I go they telling me nobody name so working here . . . No no no, Harry boy! You taking all de *joy* out my life.

Last place I try, I know I fooling m'self or is you fooling me, cause was plain-as-could-be. Was that stone quarry in Jersey. The men ask me who is me. They tell me where I could find you but they give me a far direction. And I was walking and knowing was de wrong-way I going over them rocks, over that *long* track and them stones to de back. So when I reach there and nobody there? I wasn't surprise.

Is de same pattern how it happen in too much places. But of all my disappointment, that stone quarry was de worse. Cause when I get back and tell de boss-man who send me that if you there I ain't see you, and he curse and say, *"Damn that dude. Done disappeared, did he? Wonder why he did that?"* I just know to my bosom that de man know something . . .

"Did he know you were coming," he ask me, and I tell him you couldn't know I was coming or else you wouldn't be running. I tell him you don't even know I in America. *"If he did know I here, he would be looking f'me, mister,"* I tell de man. And they all laugh-out in one big-shout . . .

At me! I had to ask m'self is what I say wrong? I just couldn't stand it. And if I'da know is so it would be, I never woulda gone. Harold, I leave that place feeling sad and small. Wondering if you working there in truth . . . if you really running from me.

From all I could see, de same thing happening in too many places and I could look in de faces of de people I meeting and tell . . . Harold, you running from me? But why? How you could running from me? Is what I do you?

But know what? Is come a time when you can't take it no more . . . Is that time you try you try you try you try!

Aye!

You try everything possible to get out your hole, but nothing doing. Them is de times you does have to stop and take-stock-of-your-life. Them is de times — and God help de life them times does come too often in. Cause they ain't easy. They ain't easy at all at all — them is de times that does make people *mad!*

I remember that nice man, Mr. Hudson, that American black man. I use to work for him and his wife in Guyana. Sometimes I would find m'self just left my work and loss listening to he talk bout America . . . But I didn't believe he.

A time his wife want to go away to America. He

say: *"For what, sweetie?"* And just then de telephone ring. *"Hey, Woodie,"* he say to his friend calling from America. *"She says she wants to leave here to go there. Tell my wife to stay where she is, will you? Can you believe her? . . . Here, talk to Woodie, sweetheart, maybe he can convince you. Hell! I married a nut!"*

I wonder is where Mr. Hudson is now? Clarise say to herself. He was a nice man, but his wife? She was lil giddy giddy. She did fire me . . .

Justso!

Ohhh, no! I don't ever want to remember! Is times like *that* does try my soul. Times like that I talking bout . . . Mr. Hudson did write a book and then I never hear nothing more. I stop working for them . . .

I wonder where he is, if they still together? Ow, he was a nice man . . . But I couldn't understand is what he was talking bout, how two coconut-tree in a yard with some grass could be nicer than them nice nice place I use to see pon de matinee screen? Big-house, yes, and servant, cause everybody can't afford that . . . but grass?

I say to m'self is what-de-ass he talking bout? Look them long long motorcar and furnitures and clothes and so they have in America? So is why me must *glad* to walk from BV to come to they house every day to see more grass and coconut-tree? I did much rather be . . .

In America . . .

Me? I did want to come here so bad I did planning to ask him if he could get a visa f'me so I could come and send for Harold. And I would done it! Ain't nothing woulda stop me from sending f'he. Nutting nutting nutting coulda sway me from that. But y'see he Harold? Men could forget . . . We women stronger. We vows does last longer . . .

Eh-eh!

But before I could get de chance to talk to de man? She fire me! He woulda never do that!

But a day he proper cuss me! He gimme a *taa-laa* abusing I will *never* forget it . . .

Was a day when he was pon de phone to de prime minister and de lady-nextdoor, living downstairs in de servant quarters keeping de house till de American Lutheran minister come back, say that she want to call her husband. She ask me if I could please ask she-de-Madam-Mistress-Hudson if she could allow her (de lady-nextdoor) to use de phone to call her husband before he leave work 'leven-o'clock, cause she want to ask him to bring home something. But de madam say:

"Mr. Hudson is on the phone to the P.M. She'll have to wait."

Eh-eh!

Ten-thirty, ten-forty, quarter-to-'leven!

De lady-nextdoor anxious, so I go to she-de-Miz-Hudson and say, *"Ma'am? Mr. Hudson still pon de phone? De lady-nextdoor want to use it. She still waiting. She have to catch her husband before 'leven-o'clock!"*

"Clarise," Miz Hudson say to me, *"she'll have to wait. He's talking to the prime minister."*

Yes, I say to m'self, but prime minister have to got conscience too. I know Mr. Hudson have much more than *she* cause like cockroach eat out she conscience . . .

Eh-eh! Ten-to-'leven! I go back to she:

"Ma'am, de lady-nextdoor —" Before I could finish my words she pounce pon me.

Jeez!

"Clarise, leave me alone, please! I have nothing more to say on that subject. Mr. Hudson is still speaking to

the prime minister and I'm not going to interrupt him."
    Steewpps!
    She was *too* constipated with herself. I just decide
that I don't have to tell her a word, that she don't got to
give me no permission, and I finding m'self right-up
there? Rap on de door and tell that *nice* Mr. Hudson . . .
    "De lady-nextdoor waiting pon de phone, sir!"
    Ow!
    But he proper bump me that day. God! I never see
a man fly into such a beautiful rage before. Is so I stand-
up by de door watching he. He was a big-tall man with
a lil big-belly but he had de height and size to carry it.
He had black-and-white hair-and-beard and he had two
eyes like red-hot coalbrick, them real burning coals, not
no kiln-coal. Them coal what y'have to fell mora-tree to
get, solid and full of fire-and-heat and slow slow burning. Is so Mr. Hudson eye did stay and I *shiver* when
he press it pon me that day and say:
    *"Excuse me, Prime Minister, please forgive me for
one second."* And he clamp a solid palm pon de phone-
mouth and he say, *"Clarise! Who the* fuck *pays your
salary? The lady next door?"*
    Yet? Yet he woulda *never* fire me. I *know* that . . .
But she?
    De day she fire me his good friend Mr. Hart, a art-
ist, was visiting him from America and I hear good what
they say to one-another so she or me can't hear. But if
is *one* thing I know I have is two good ears . . .
    He say:
    *"Tom, old buddy, you remember Ghana? Remem-
ber Sack-'em-Lena? Well, old buddy, your ace come to
Guyana and married one just like her — Lena. She don't
take no shit off nobody! But I kinda liked Clarise. She's*

a nut! Know what she did?" And Mr. Hudson tell Mr. Hart the story bout the phone call that day and when he finish he say: *"It's a wonder old Sack-'em-Lena didn't send her packing* that *time."*

And when I hear that? I know he did forgive me. Is only she . . .

I wonder where he?

Ow, but if they did *only* listen to that man, eh? If they did only listen . . .

I remember de day he say Guyana facing a crisis. I will *never* forget that day, cause everybody was talking them days bout how we going *Feed House and Clothe Ourselves by 1976.* And he? Mr. Hudson? Is what he talking? He ringing up de phone and talking to somebody when he say it:

"Kit! We ought to call a special meeting to discuss some things. I've been talking to my gardener all morning. I'm putting some things together . . ."

I was cooking in de kitchen and I listen him, cause I use to listen to everything he say and a lot of it like that day use to sound like if he talking miracles or he have to be a see-far man or something . . . Or else he mad . . . He talk bout Ghana, when he working there, then he say:

"Guyana is facing a crisis!"

And by afternoon?

Eh-eh! De house full of people cause like de word spread round de place that Mr. Hudson say Guyana facing a crisis and some of his American friends who working in Guyana too come to hear for theyself how he could think Guyana facing this crisis. They want to know, cause like they don't want to go back to America. I couldn't understand what was wrong with them people. How they could prefer to stay in Guyana than to be

172

in America. I was sorry I couldn't wait to hear what he had to say but I had to hustle home to prepare Harold and them children dinner. I didn't want them waiting pon me . . .

I wonder where he, Mr. Hudson?

De people say he did leave de country cause they stop listening he. They say he was *mad,* drunk, all kind of things, cause they couldn't see so far to right here where we is, there in Guyana right now . . .

Ow! I wonder where is he. Cause I got to cut a sirihi in my life right now in America. I got to get away, go home, now now now! But how? If I could only find Mr. Hudson . . . I hear he leave de country a very sad man cause they stop listening he . . .

Is what was wrong with we? Is what did do me, that I couldn't see what he was saying?

"Tell my wife, Woodie. Talk to her . . . She wants to leave here to go there . . ." I wonder where she?

Steewpps! She did properly constipate . . . But wait! It have a directory here, behind this chair. I will look for his name in de directory and see if —

BLAPS!

Is Clarise dusting dusting with a feathermop at her cleaning-job at the antiquestore, dreaming as usual, and, BLAPS! A nice teacup fall down and break.

Eh-eh!

Is so Clarise left watching the thing pon the floor and cussing herself:

Ow, Clarise, is why you so clumsy with y'self? Now look how you break de people nice nice teacup. You going have to pay for de thing this guava-season when you don't even have a cent to save-de-dog-flea-from-de-gallows. But you self, Clarise, you is a big-woman, not a chile . . .

Clarise pick up a piece of the teacup. Only yester-day Mr. Jacobson tell her to take the things come from Hong Kong out the case with the straw and put them on the shelves and he tell her to be careful . . . And now she break one of the *nicest* teacups.

I wonder is how much it cost? Mustbe a three dol-lar? Four or five dollar? Y'will have to pay for it, Clarise! Ow Lawd! This is *real* ole-house-pon-ole-house this good day! *This* is one them times! Is what you going do if they *fire* you, eh? You can't ask Mavis now to carry you pon her back again till you find more work . . . And you was just thinking you would look for a place to go pon your own with de lil money you manage to save. And go home. You ain't got de passage, but y'was get-ting close and everything now . . . Lawd! Is why trou-bles don't come single?

"Clarise . . . *Clarise* . . . CLARISE!"

"Ohhh . . . yes, sir! I sorry . . . My mind was wandering."

Clarise surprise! The man, the boss, the antique-store-owner catch her with his break-up teacup in her hand, and watch! He bending down. He picking up — a *glass,* too? Is all that break? Ow Lawd, save me! That mustbe another five-six dollars . . .

Clarise didn't even realize that typewriter and all them other noisy machines in the place stop, and is everybody left so staring at she and watching what going on.

"What is it? What is it, Henry?"

Is the boss wife running coming now. She have a office in the antiquestore, too.

I can't stand this woman, Lawd! Clarise saying in her mind. She does treat me like if . . . like if I ain't got no *right* to breathing de same air with she. De man would give me a chance, but she *bound* to make —

"Oh my God! That's a piece from the new ship-ment that just came in from — *Ohhh my God!*"

Y'see? Y'see? Y'see? Is me she don't like. Now she *got* me! Is de boss wife. Is she start already. Watch how that woman getting-on over a lil cup-to-drink-tea-in. She going make me lose my job over a lil cup-to-drink-tea-in?

"Okay, Martha, calm down, will you?"

Is her husband trying to talk sense in her head.

"But Henry, that was a complete set. And the vase, that cut-glass vase. The Moynihans ordered that for — We can't get another one in time!"

One lil teacup and a vase? Is how people could get-on so over stupidness so? All they have to do is buy the thing back . . . But no! This woman want me lose my job, is that, is nothing but that. But ain't she a woman like me? She can't have more sympathy? She ain't got to go to no university, she ain't got to be no see-far woman to know, to see I po'. She could just *look* at me and see. I want this work. I need it . . . baaad! It ain't nothing much, but is *all* I got . . .

Go, Clarise, go and get money to pay, or else you going lose this job today today.

Clarise start to walk away.

"Clarise! Come back here!"

"I coming in a minute, sir."

Clarise go to the room near where they have the coffeepot. Steewpps! People does drink too much coffee in this country. Since I small my mother use to tell me that too much coffee does make you *dunce*. Clarise fret-ting to herself.

Clarise come back with her ole brown purse Mavis give her that does hold plenty things. Clarise take out her bread-and-fish wrap up in a piece of foilpaper. She take out her kerchief and a ole fold-up bus-transfer fall out. Clarise pick it up quick from dirtying-up the floor. She take out a green meshbag that she was going use later on to buy groceries to take home in and a small paperbag.

She searching for a small-change-purse with her money fold-up inside it. And she talking all the time. She talking fast fast so that *that spiteful woman* won't get a chance to harden her husband heart:

"Sir? I don't have much money now, but I would hope that you would take de money out my pay, sir. But if you want payment now, sir? I have it *right here!* Wait, sir! Just now I will find it . . . *Steewpps!* This bag could hold plenty things but it *too* confuse! Eh-eh! Look how I messing-up de place! . . . Wait! Yes . . . look, it here!"

Clarise hitch her big-purse under her shoulder and is so she opening the small-change-purse quick quick and she pulling out the fold-up money . . . a five-dollar-bill look like it see better days . . . three dollar-bills . . . some change . . .

"Look, sir, is so much for it? Is how much for it, sir? I *know* you will understand and give me a chance if I pay for it. Is how much for it, eh?"

Eh-eh! Is what do that woman, eh? Like she going catch *fits* or something? They better put spoon in her mouth quick before she bite her tongue. Is choke she choking? Eh-eh!

"Martha!" the man say. "Why don't you go to your office and let me settle this?"

"But Henry! Do you realize what has happened here? This woman does not *understand* the *value* of these things. How could she have worked here for *all these months* and she doesn't even know the *value* of anything? She's *dangerous*, Henry!"

Eh-eh! Is what these people talking bout at all? Me? Clarise? Dangerous? I never lift my hand to a soul . . . Well, that time with Leonie was different. I did have to learn her a lesson. But that was different . . . I never harm a *fly* in my life. Is what these people talking bout I *dangerous*?

"Yes, Martha, I know, but let me handle it."

"But Henry . . ."

"Okay, Martha, *you* handle it!"

Ohhh, Jesus Lawd, I ask for mercy . . .

"No, sir! Take de money! I will give you *six* dollars . . . is nearly *all* I have. *Take* it! I will buy my token with this dollar and I will buy a lil grind-beef with de rest for dinner. Take it! Take it! *Take all* . . ."

Is so Clarise going crazy shoving the money in the man hand.

"Weren't you told these were expensive things?" he say.

"Yes, sir . . ."

"How much were you told they cost? Who told you?"

"Mr. Jacobson, sir."

The boss look round at the people looking on and he ask:

"Where is Jacobson, is he here?"

Clarise boss peeping round the people watching in the office looking for Mr. Jacobson who is the manager of the place. Is he that hire Clarise. Somebody say:

"He's out to lunch!"

"He *must* be, to have hired this woman," the boss wife say. And Clarise now know in truth that the woman constipate, cause is what Mr. Jacobson hiring her have to do with he going out for he lunch, eh?

177

"Well, what did Mr. Jacobson say to you? Tell me," the boss say.

"He say I must be careful cause the wares cost thousands of dollars."

"The wares? . . . Anyway, what about the crystal?"

"What crystal, sir?"

The boss walk over to a case and pick up a glass like the vase that break. He hold it up to Clarise and the light catch it. "What about *this*?" he say.

It make Clarise remember the pork-knocker they call Burst-and-Scatter. He and her father was friends but Clarise daddy never had luck like Burst-and-Scatter. They use to prospect in the bush together. They call him Burst-and-Scatter after the name he name his boat, a big flat-bottom boat that he make heself and high-water-or-low, in-and-outa-season, sometimes with only *one* man, his nephew, or whosoever else ain't frighten the punishment and he get them to follow him over all them bad-falls, you would see him yakking-paddle round them bends in the river, going Ireng, Siparuni, Cuyuni, anywhere he feel to go looking for gold.

That man have mind, hear? And when he come back to landing? He coming with the living thing.

Mac, that his other name, his real name, Clarise say to herself. Mac *always* making. Then he going drink through. High-wine like *water* for *days* till his money done . . . But that is not de point . . .

One day Burst-and-Scatter come back from a trip. He been away for months and he come back with a nice set of diamonds that he find in a ole tacomba at Millionaire Creek in Kurupung, and Clarise see it. She was spending time up there with her father and she remem-

178

ber the dirty stones still full of mud from the creek and wrap-up in brown paper.

Unpolish diamonds.

Clarise was bout twelve or thirteen years old and she remember thinking to herself, All that punishment through all them bad-falls risk drowning and snake-and-tiger in de bush for months and months? And *that* is all? And she run away to play.

But her daddy call her back and say:

"Come see what under all de dirt, children," and he and Burst-and-Scatter show Clarise and her brother a real big polish diamond. Is justso the light was shining and pointing at her like that vase in the boss hand. But that wasn't no glass. That was a diamond. A *real* diamond . . .

"I know, sir. It nice, sir. That is why I willing to pay for it, sir. That is why I giving you all my money to pay for it . . . If I giving you overs you can give me back de change . . . If it need a lil more you can take it out my pay . . ."

The boss wife groan and start to cry and just when he turning to tell her something else she walk away wiping her eye.

Is why she have to crying over a lil teacup and a vase that I begging them to pay for, eh? Clarise saying in her mind. In Guyana one like that expensive now, but that is only cause everything gone up. I know to my *breast* that here in America that thing can't cost more than a lil four-five dollars and de vase a lil more than that. And *that* is too much for anybody to pay for a tea-cup, especially somebody who po'-like-church-rat like me . . . But is me that break it, so is me that have to pay for it. So what is all de fussing-and-crying bout? . . .

Well, Clarise girl, you do your best, and it look like they want you to get pon your knees now, and that is what you not going do in this life, no! So just answer they reasonable questions and shut up, Clarise.

Don't beg, Clarise!

You may end up roaming de streets again looking for another job. You may end up in de po'-house or stone-cold-dead, but till then you will walk with your self-respect. Don't let them take that away from you, girl . . . If they want to fire you, let them fire you onetime. Just *don't beg*, Clarise.

"Did Mr. Jacobson tell you that something like this is very valuable?"

"Yes, sir. That's why I'm giving you *all* I have to pay for it."

And the man just fire her.

Thirteen

BLAPS!

Justso! De thing just fall down and break . . . de stupid teacup ain't even know what it *do* to me justso . . . It go and break! Now, watch me! Alone in this America. Can't find my man don't even know where he gone, where he . . .

Ohhhhh! HARReeeeeeeeeeeeee!

Is Clarise walking the streets again. Loss-away again when a voice call out her name:

"Clarise! Clarise Cumberbatch! Look, over here, it's me . . . Look! Over here. Still looking for your fella?"

"Bella!"

"Yes, sister . . . I got a lead . . . Take the number five from down there, right? Over there, see? . . . Go down there and look for the *number five*. When you get to Franklin, get off, cross the platform . . . get off, yes,

that's right . . . cross the platform . . . take a *number
two* — that'll be the local. It'll take you to Newkirk . . .
That's it, sister, your stop! Oh! Take the *back* of that
train . . . part that leaves the platform last! When you
get off at Newkirk, there'll be an exit. You'll see it right
there . . . Take it out to the streets. Sometimes, eve-
nings, there's some good fish on sale right there. When
you get up the stairs? Right there, make a left. Go one
block . . ."

By the time she get to Newark Avenue, Clarise breathing hard hard . . .
    But Clarise? Is not you say you don't care no more?
How come you here? How come you killing y'self running going looking for Harold Cumberbatch?
    But is *Bella* say . . . She say it have a man *defi-
nitely* know where Harold is, and he living in this place
. . . Bella say go . . . and that Mavis did know!
    No! *All this time* Mavis did know?
    Mavis did know, she did know she did know.
    Ow God! She did know! How Mavis coulda do that
to meeeee? Then call herself my-sister-my-friend! Take-
me-in-lend-me-money! And she did know is where is
Harold *all this time*?
    Ow, Mavis!
    Owowowowowowowowowowowowowowowowow!
    Ow!
    Ow, Mavis! . . .
    "*When you get under that window, call out, Andy!
three times . . . On the third call if someone doesn't
answer, means nobody's there. Be careful — ain't the
easiest neighborhood over there . . . But Clarise? Are
you sure you want to do this? Are you ready to meet
that man again? Suppose he ain't the —*"

182

"Bella, I always ready, no matter what I say to m'self, I always ready to talk to Harold . . ."

But you lie to Bella. You lie, Clarise, y'lie y'lie, you lying to yourself.

Yes, I lie, I lie I lie *I lie-like-a-ass!* Lawd! Is four-years-and-more! . . .

Is what I going say to him?

Is what he thinking?

Is what he pass through?

Is who he is now?

He can't be de same Harold. Look me, I come to America one year and I ain't de same Clarise. I lie! I ain't ready . . . I ain't ready . . .

Clarise reach the place and she start to call out:

"ANDY!"

". . . Let about three minutes pass . . . count quickly to three hundred between each call . . ."

Clarise counting and calling out:

"ANDY!" . . . two hundred and eighty-nine . . . two hundred and — "SHIT!" she say. Too impatient to wait any longer, Clarise scream out: "ANDEEE!"

"Okay!"

Is a window raise up.

Is a head push out.

Is a voice answer her:

"You sound legit. Stop that *confounded bellowing,* now, and come on up . . . fifth floor. Make it quick. I've got to go. I'm in a hurry . . ."

Is a man talk so . . .

Is who?

"Oh, by the way, do I know you? Are you here to —"

"Is Harold Cumberbatch I come to. Is his wife, Clarise Cumber —"

BLAM!

Is de window slam down.

"No, mister, *no!*" Clarise say. "Not this time. I ain't gone from here till I know . . ."

Is what de man did say? . . . Foots, don't fail me now, please . . . Gimme more walk, gimme more —

Run, Clarise, run! Is only one elevator these buildings does have. He have to come-out that. Watch de entrance there and —

Eh-eh!

Children! No more than *boys,* fourteen-fifteen-sixteen years ole . . . Watch how them block up de entranceway! How them smoke de dope! Hear how them cuss-like-coolie! Ow, me! Children should be in *school* this hour-de-day, not idle bout de place so . . . Go slow, girl . . . Don't excite them . . . Go careful through them, chile, and *smile* and say

"Mawning!"

"*Good* morning, mums!"

Ow Lawd! Thanks, Lawd! They ain't hurt you, chile, and *please* protect my children, my daughter Eunice and my son Clarence. Please please please. *Keep* them for me till I come. I begging you, God, for *my* sake, spare them, keep them . . . till I come . . .

Look de elevator, here it coming now . . . Get in . . .

Is a man inside . . .

"Mister, good mawning! You could please press number five floor for me, please?"

The man press the button and the door closing and he only staring . . .

Eh-eh!

But is where we going?

Lawd Jesus! Is down de elevator going down?

BUMP!

"Here's where you get off, bitch!"

184

"Me? Mister? Oh, no! Here is not where I going, like you press de wrong button . . . And here is where? Is not down? Is not de basement? I going up, sir, to Andy! You know he?"

"I know *you*, bitch, and don't give me no —"

WOP!

BOP!

"Ayeeeeee!"

"Owowowowowowowooouch! You HIT me, mister! MISTER, IS WHAT I DO YOU? IS WHERE YOU DRAGGING ME GOING? MISTER, YOU WRONG! I DON'T KNOW YOU. YOU DON'T KNOW ME. MISTER, YOU HURTING MY —"

POW!

"OOWWWW! BUT I AIN'T COME FROM HERE, I TRYING TO MAKE YOU SEE . . . IS NOT ME YOU LOOKING FOR . . . IS WHERE YOU DRAGGING ME? OW, SIR, YOU MAKING A BIG MISTAKE!"

"Shut up, *bitch!*"

BOPOPBOW!

POW!

"UGH!"

He throw-you-down, Clarise. You hurt your head? Yes!

And de pain jook me where I hit my head. But I can't afford to die. NOT NOW! Ohhh, Lawd! Is lights is lights is lights in my head. I GOING . . . DIE! Ohhhhh! What's this what's this what's this? He-got-you-by-de-collar.

He choking you . . . Is why you don't holler? He dragging you pon this pissy pissy floor. Like your mind going numb numb numb. Is-de-pain-in-de-head. Is-de-lightning. Light . . . ning . . . Light . . . ning-ning . . .

Ning-ning . . .

You seeing *ningning*, Clarise. Don't go out — open your mouth and *bawl!*

BAWL, girl, bawl! Somebody down-de-hall bound to hear you. Ow! But . . . then . . . he . . .

going . . .

Kill you! . . . Is what he doing? Open your eye. Open it — LOOK! He zipping-down-he-fly-don't-open-your-eye-*too*-big . . . Look! Is-zipping-down-he-zip-ping-down . . .

And *look!* How he trembl . . . ing . . . ningning! Think, girl think . . . forget de pain . . . that man going *kill* you this good day if you don't THINK, girl, think! . . . What is your name? . . . What is your . . . Clarise! Clarise who? . . . Ow-my-God! . . . Ow-my-God! OW ME!

He *see* me looking at he . . . Now . . . he going . . . KICK! . . . me . . . straight pon . . . oowwww! Ohhhhh . . . nooooo! . . . Play-a-game-play-a-game-play-a-game-with-y'self . . . Call-y'name-call-y'name . . . Ohhh! . . . De pain. De-pain-o-de-pain-o. Clarise-is-m'name-Clarise-is-m'name-Clarise-is-y'name-Clarise-is-m'name . . . Owwwohhh! What? Which . . . is de way?

Which-which-which-is . . .

Ohhhhh!

Nooooo!

Is-times-like-these-is-times-like-these . . .

If-I-did-hear-what-Miz-Goring-say-I-won't-a-been-in-this-mess-today . . .

But Clarise, is how you come to lay-down flat pon your back in this stinking hole? . . . Waiting . . . F'what? Go, Clarise chile . . .

No! You *have* to get-up-and-go, girl. Is time to GETUPANDGO!

"I'm gonna fix you, bitch."

Watch he coming down pon you with he crotch expose. Is what he going do? Is what wrong with you? You *must* have some strength left . . . Find it! And *kick* he! Right *there,* y'see?

Now! DISH-IT-IN-HE!

Booooeuuf! Bup!

Hawahumhawhumhawwaaahhhhh!

"You bawling?"

"Aaagghh!"

"You bawling? Y'bawling? Well *bawl* if y'bawling cause if I could only find de strength I going kick you with these two big-shoes right there again . . ."

Ow! But he *proper* maul-up. Your skin, chile.

But watch how he holding he crotch and bawling. *I will kick he again,* let he bawl some mo —

NO! Clarise, y'fool. *Getupandgo!* Watch how he hopping pon one foot with all-two-hand-clap-pon-he-crotch bawling like babboon in de jungle. Look how he pants going trip he . . . No! Don't wait, girl.

You just . . . kick him over . . . and . . . GET-UPANDGO!

CLARISE, GO! Cause he going *kill* you if he catch you.

Get! . . .

De pain de pain de pain . . .

UP!

Owowowowowow! . . .

GO!

Ohhhhh . . . pleeease . . . ow! De pain de pain de pain. Which is de way? Which is de way out? Is where de elevator? Is where de door? Where . . . de . . . doooor . . . ohhhhh!

Nooooo! Pleeease! No no no NO . . . MORE!

Fourteen

How do you keep the music playing?
How do you make it last?
How do you keep the song from fading too fast?
How do you lose yourself to someone and never lose
* your way?*
How do you not run out of new things to say?
And since we know we're always changing, how can it
* be the same? . . .*

Clarise hearing the words of a sweet sweet song a
man and a woman singing and they coming from a distance and getting closer and . . . closer, till they right
in her ears in the room pon a stereo . . .
  Where?
  Is where you, Clarise?
  Pon a bed! Clean sheet! Nightdress? This is not

yours . . . and a dressing-case like Mavis . . . But is
not Mavis own? Is you alone? No . . . a man . . . is . . .

"Mr. *Grimes?*"

"Yes, Clarise. How are you today? Feeling better
now?"

"Yes, but how . . . ?"

"It's a long story. Look, I'm making you some food,
real food, not just soup. You've been living on soup for
five days . . ."

FIVE DAYS!

WHERE?

"Where is here?"

"My home, my apartment. You came —"

"Andy!"

"That's me."

"Harold?"

"He's gone."

"Oh?"

"That's all you have to say, just 'oh'?"

"Gone where?"

"We'll talk later. Now I want you to get out of that
bed and prepare to eat a meal. I'm cooking it myself.
Paella! Especially for you."

"But how . . . ?"

"We'll talk over dinner. Come now. How do you
feel? Good enough to get up?"

"Yes . . ."

"Or you can rest longer. I could bring the feast in
here. Look, over there? A table —"

"No, I will get up, Mr. Grimes."

"Andy . . . call me Andy. You spent a long enough
time with me to call me Andy . . . And you are Clarise."

"I leave all my things at Mavis . . ."

"She knows, I have them here. But I bought you some new —"

"Who tell her?"

"I did. She came to see you. She cried . . . you slept on . . . She loves you . . ."

"Harold? Where Harold?"

"He's in Washington, D.C."

"What he say bout me? He know I here?"

"No, before he knew it was you he had escaped, there, by the fire es —"

"Escape? But why? Why he want to *escape* from me?"

"He . . . I . . . he thought you were Leonie. I told him you were coming up . . . Incidentally, the man who did this to you had to be taken to hospital. They found him in the basement with a ruptured —"

"He wanted to kill me!"

"Yes, I know, you were lucky. You are a very strong woman, but mostly lucky. Quite a few rape victims in this building identified him. At least one woman he must have assaulted didn't live to tell the tale. You were lucky."

"How Harold?"

"Not very well."

"Why? He sick? What happen to him?"

"In the mind. He's not a very happy man . . . But let me leave you to bathe or shower . . . There! And here you have some clothes. Mavis helped me choose them for you. Come out when you're through."

A wardrobe! Open it, Clarise, open it . . .

Inside?

A nice dressing-gown with lil feathers at de collar and round de nice flare-sleeves. Nice *bright* color, too, like wild-somatoo and . . .

Touch it, Clarise, touch it!

Aye!

Soft-and-nice!

Ow, Clarise girl, this would look *nice* on you. Go to de mirror . . . is a long nice one, eh? On de wall near de bathroom door . . .

Ohhh, lovely!

Eh-eh! Clarise girl? Is *you* who could wear this? But first, watch y'self! Look your hair how it cassy cassy, watch de . . . But you look clean! Is how you look so clean?

Eh-eh!

Five days! And you ain't even — Lemme see . . . smelling, self? Somebody had to cleaning you . . . But who?

Andrew Grimes!

What is this!

And what is this?

Is his *pajama* you have on? His pajama-top? . . .

"That belongs to Harold." Andrew Grimes stick his head in the door. "You called his name in your sleep all the time at first, before you became rested late yesterday . . ."

"This? Harold own? Is a nice one . . ."

"I'm sorry I interrupted you, but I saw you through the door. Do you like it — the dressing gown, I mean? In your hand, Clarise. I couldn't help saying, 'That would look just fine on her.' "

"Yes, but —"

"Then put it on! And hurry, dinner will be ready in a minute. There's a shower massage . . ."

Go in the bathroom, Clarise, go.

Eh-eh!

Look this big big bouquet of flowers! And a card!

"For Clarise . . ."

Eh-eh! And inside it?
"On your recovery."
From?
Andy!
Eh-eh!
And is bath-oil-and-beads and heartshape-soap and
bubblebath and towel with CC mark pon it and pon de
soap, too . . .
All for you?
Eh-eh!
Wash your skin, Clarise chile. Get under de shower,
girl, bathe your skin with a piece of soap. What is this?
Shower? Massage? Is fat-water *boring-up de skin* . . .
Feel like if you just come from playing in de waves and
you get a falls-massage . . .
One of de towels . . . Where it is? . . . Use it . . .
Rub your body with de towel, Clarise. Rub it rub it rub.
Ouch!
Now look! look at your body . . . How you look,
chile?
Sturdy!
Look at your face.
Peaceful and calm and nice . . .
WINK!
Is how *you,* chile?
Alive-and-kicking!
Well you is a *real* mule, chile. Y'is a *horse.* Cause
with all that *carracking* your body get? If you still here
cracking? You is a . . .

> gallop f'me, horse
> gallop f'me . . .

Now, Clarise girl! You have to go outside and find
out what next. Don't even *guess.* Just go! You going

soon know how this one happen . . . But first, comb your hair. Your Afro need cutting. And clean your teeth. Thank God is still all yours, cause that was a *brutalizing* you get there . . . You going have this *bruise* pon your neck . . .

But nevermind! Put on lil deodorant, this fancy slipper here, and . . .

Eh-eh!

Is you look so good, Clarise! Is *you*?

Well go now, girl. Go!

"*There* you are! You look ab-so-lutely *enchanting!* You know that?"

"I know I look better than I look when I come here and I feel a hundred times better . . . Thanks. But what happen?"

"Sit here. I'll tell you all about it over dinner. Have you ever had paella?"

"No."

"But I bet you've eaten pilau?"

"Oh, yes! Is de same as cook-up, not so?"

"I think so, only a little more elaborate. It's a mixture of seafood . . . crab, lobster, shrimp, clams — anything from the sea. A little saffron, see? That's what gives it this nice *yellow* color, and of course there's meat in it too, like — But you don't want to learn recipes now, you want to hear what happened to you, isn't that so?"

"Yes, and —"

"You were almost *raped*, you know that?"

"Yes, I get away . . ."

"You not only got away, you defended yourself quite well. The police ought to be very grateful to you. He must have heard me speak to you through the window."

"Yes, mustbe that. But . . . wait! You say Harold

thought was Leonie, but I *tell* you I was Clarise before. You didn't tell Harold? Why?"

"Tell him what?"

"That was not Leonie but me."

"I didn't hear you say your name."

He lying, Clarise, he lie! That window slam down too fast. That face remove in too much of a hurry. But don't worry, chile, don't worry . . . And don't hurry, either. Take it cool . . . cool breeze . . . Remember, your mission tonight is to find-out de *whole* story . . . So don't-rock-de-boat, girl, don't-rock-de-boat . . .

"Anyway, you ruptured him good — Probably put him out of commission for life, poor man."

"Poor man? Poor man? Is how you could call a man like that poor man? You know where he had me? Flat-down pon my back on that nasty stinking basement floor with my foot-skin open . . . He deserve all he get! Is *poor* you call he? But allyuh men is something, yes! I say is good for he! Now he have to wait for somebody to bugger he. But he ain't even going get that, cause any man who would rape-down woman so ain't going stand-up still for *nobody* —"

Clarise stop talking sudden and she saying in her mind:

Steewpps! Clarise, just shut-up-your-mouth, hear? You come here to buy milk, not to reckon cow!

"Mister, I talk too much, I talking too much . . . I never talk so with . . ."

"That means you're feeling better, and I'm glad. I've done everything I could think of to make you comfortable since you fell into my arms in the basement. I went looking for you, you know. I was afraid when you didn't come upstairs that something like this might have happened. You were lucky . . . I called up my friend

194

Pauline — she's a gynecologist. She examined you . . .
said you hadn't been touched, except externally, of
course. She said you were suffering from exhaustion
and that you needed complete bedrest for as long as the
sedative she prescribed lasted. Said I should see that
the dose was strictly administered down to the time —
which is right now."

Andrew Grimes open his palm and show Clarise
two capsules.

"There are only two left. You should take one now,
and one tomorrow morning. Then you can get up and
go out into the world again."

"I —" Clarise open her mouth to say something but
Andrew Grimes stop her.

"Wait! Pauline said that even *then,* when you're
ready to go out again, I should try to persuade you to
rest a little longer. But if you insist on leaving, you should
take it easy. She said you must stay calm or you'll risk
a nervous breakdown. You must have been through a
lot even before your little encounter downstairs."

"Ohhh! Oh-oh-oh-ohhh! Mister? If you only know,
if you only know, if I could tell you what I pass through
. . . But I feel like if it over now. Must be de sleep or
something . . . My body, my mind feel lighter, though
I still have a weariness in me somewhere, y'know what
I mean? Like a . . . wondering what to do . . ."

"I bathed you, you know . . ." Mr. Grimes start to
say.

"Oh, was you!"

"Yes, I touched your body . . . you called out his
name . . . Harold!"

"Ohhhhh!"

"Please, please don't say it like that. Don't look that
way, Clarise. I didn't defile your body. I promise you, all

I did was worship you . . . I wish . . . I wish I were a painter, a poet. Then I could express . . . make you see how I felt, how I feel right now . . ." Andrew Grimes saying to Clarise and she saying to herself:

Clarise? You burning-up, girl. You got de feelings all up you . . .

"Begging your pardon, please, mister . . ."

"Andy, say Andy, please."

"Andy . . ."

"Yes, Clarise, what is it?"

"You didn't have no right to do that, y'know?"

"To do what? To bathe you? Okay, but then who? Who would have done it? Mavis refused to take care of you while you were sedated. And what's more, she cautioned me in her *foulest Guyanese language*. We're old antagonists, you know. She has always hated my guts."

"She thought y'was a headhunter."

"I know. About two years ago she saw me with your husband at the OTB place on Forty-second Street. She accosted him and let out a tirade on him for deserting you and for associating with me, a headhunter, *chicken hawk*, I think was the word she used. She's not the only one's mistaken my . . .

"But anyway, here I was, alone with you. What was I to do? And here you are still, Clarise," he say, breathing hard and looking at her. "I want to touch you again. I want to see your naked body again when you're awake, conscious . . . I want you to want me . . ."

"Ohhh stop!" He have to stop, Lawd! I can't stand this, Clarise say to herself.

But is why you have to *stand* it, Clarise? Is why you don't just free-up y'self? Just let go de feelings, chile. They been store-up inside you too long . . . all these years . . . Free-up, free-up, free-up y'self before you explode! Lively-up y'self, girl . . .

But first, Clarise, first find out de *whole* story . . .

"Hey! Is what you doing to me?"

"I'm making love to you, Clarise, and you *like* it . . . You like it, don't you? Please, tell me . . . tell me, tell me, tell me . . ."

"Yes, yes, YES!" Clarise say.

"Oh, Clarise, come, come, let's go . . ."

"No . . . not yet . . ."

"Why?"

"Cause . . . cause I . . . cause . . ." Clarise starting and stopping.

Is what you want to say, Clarise? *Say* it! Y'is a *big-woman* y-must know-your-mind!

"Cause I can't make a good . . . I can't sell. Wait! I will tell you a story bout a woman. A *nice* woman, a friend of mine. Not Mavis. This one living in Guyana still. She tell me that how she does go and lie-down with de men cause thing bad with she. But she don't ask them for money cause she don't want to have to think bout herself as a prosti —

" 'Well how you does get if you don't ask?' I ask my friend. 'I does hope they will be grateful and give me something out they *own conscience,*' she say.

"And she tell me how hard it is to lie-down knowing that why you really lying there is for gain, unless you like it and nobody ain't giving you good, or you is one of them who have-to-have-it, y'know what I mean? So you don't care is who or why, y'just have to try get some best way you can?

"Mister, I want to know something from you, and if you don't tell me first, all I going thinking when I lie-down with you is —"

"What do you want to know, Clarise?"

"Where is my husband?"

"*Goddamn it, woman!* Clarise, what do you want?

197

I've lived with you, taken care of you for a week. You called out his name, but it was a cry of pain. What do you want?" Andrew Grimes voice crack-up, like he crying.

Clarise say, "To *talk* to him."

"But he does not want to talk to you, Clarise. He's not interested in you. Your husband is only interested in making money, that's all."

The man words bore into her like a knife. Clarise feel a scream rising-up from her belly. It coming it coming it coming . . .

Is not tears . . .

Is not vexation . . .

Is not . . .

Is what?

It had a book use to be pon de shelf in Mr. Hudson house in Courida Park. Pon de cover it say *Don't Cry, Nigger, Scream.*

But you must be *calm,* Clarise.

Is that, Clarise say to herself.

And then she find herself listening, calm-as-ever to Andrew Grimes saying:

"He's not interested in you. As far as I know, *he doesn't care if he never sees you again.* He's not interested in Leonie, either. All he's interested in is making money."

Clarise ain't screaming yet, instead she asking:

"He say anything bout me?"

"Oh, great —" Andrew Grimes start to complain.

But Clarise stop him:

"Please tell me."

"He says you were a mistake."

You going scream now, right? You going scream! You going to scream? Clarise?

Eh-eh! No!

198

"Of *course* I was a mistake. *He* was mistake, too. But is all two o' we did have *hot-crutch* at de wedding-eve queh-queh that night. And is me-and-he end-up tumbling in de canefield that same night. That's why de ole people say is not a good thing to let children go to queh-queh, cause when they start with all they antics . . . Anyway, I was saying . . . De only difference between me and he was that he done did highschool already and I didn't even take school-leaving yet . . .

"And is *me* who had to fetch de *load*. Yes, sir! Children is a load a woman does have to fetch. We does have to fetch de load for nine months, inside we. Then when we lay-it-down, we does have to see it to de point where it could take care of itself. A woman understands that more than a man cause all he had was lil sweetness in some canefield or something, then he flick-he-thing-off and he done with that . . . But we? . . . Ow Lawd!" Clarise say. "Ow Lawd!

"So this *mistake* . . . Is so he decide to get rid of it, eh?" Clarise say.

"Clarise, please . . ." Andrew Grimes start to beg her.

And Clarise say sudden:

"Mr. Grimes, Andrew, y'see all them people who does cuss you? Run away from you? Thief-your-money-rob-you? Them *still* got to be grateful to you. Don't you worry with them. No matter what they say, what they do, they got to grateful to you. But all they seeing is de whiteman face pon you and they say that whitepeople responsible for *all* de worries in de world! And is fight they fighting back when they getting-on so to you. Mustn't worry with them, hear?

"But Mr. Grimes? . . ."

"Andrew."

"Andrew? . . ."

"Yes, Clarise?"

"You could do one last thing for me?"

"Of course. But will you answer one question first?"

"What?"

"You've changed your mind about coming to bed with me, haven't you?"

"Yes, Andy, I —"

"I knew it. Okay, what is it you want me to do, Clarise?"

"Please call-up de immigration and ask them to come here for me."

"WOMAN, ARE YOU CRAZY?"

"No, I —"

"*I can't do it!*"

"For me?"

"No! *Especially* not for you."

"I have to go home . . ."

"They will put you in jail!"

"I don't care."

"They will dump you on the first plane —"

"I know."

"What are you going to do?"

"Go home."

"And then?"

"Go to de bush."

"And do what, Clarise?"

"I can use your phone, please?"

"Of course, sure, there's one over there . . . But what . . . what are you doing? Are you calling someone else?"

"Yes."

"Who? Only an enemy would do a thing like that for you."

"He's a friend . . ."

"If he's a friend he won't do it, I tell you."

"He would do it. He tell me . . ."

Andrew Grimes walk over to her and take the phone away.

"Don't call him . . ."

"You going do it? You going *free-me-up* from this . . . this . . ."

"I will give you the passage," Andrew say.

"I don't want your money. I don't want it so."

"What's the matter with you? Why are you so stubborn, for crying out — I said I'll *give* you the passage, damn it, Clarise!"

"I don't want your money, I said."

"Okay, well, it's Harold's money then, not mine!" Andrew holler.

And Clarise say calm as ever:

"Better yet. I don't want anything from him. I —"

"Clarise!" Andrew Grimes cut her.

"— want to do my own thing." Clarise finish her sentence.

"Clarise, I *want* you," Andrew Grimes say.

"I'm sorry," Clarise say.

"What are you going to do for a man?"

"I . . . You might not believe this story, but I sure if you ask any bushwoman she *bound* to tell you . . . Sometimes? All y'does have to do is go and sit-down on de rocks at de foot of de waterfall and open your legs, sir, and . . ."

"Dear God! Clarise, Clarise, Clarise. I'm jealous, you've got me jealous of a water —"

"You going call?"

"Yes, Clarise. I will call immigration for you."

"Thanks, Andy . . . Tell them: My-name-is-Clarise-Cumberbatch-I-come-from-Guyana-and-I-doesn't-have-greencard!"

Hurrah!